# THE RUNT

Mike was Big Red's son, but he hardly looked or acted like the son of a champion. He was a runt, a misfit, and a general all-around mutton-head. Always wanting his own way, he never gave an inch to anyone or anything that might stand in his way. He would be worthless unless he developed some brains and showed some willingness to cooperate.

Then Danny and Mike were caught in a snow-storm on Tower Head and tracked by a puma. And Mike proved his courage and loyalty in a test that would bind him firmly to Danny for the rest of his life.

"This is a worthy sequel to *Big Red* . . . a rousing good story. Mr. Kjelgaard interprets the out-of-doors and the relationship between man and animals with understanding and mastery."
—*Library Journal*

# Irish Red
## by Jim Kjelgaard

A BANTAM SKYLARK BOOK®
TORONTO · NEW YORK · LONDON · SYDNEY · AUCKLAND

*This low-priced Bantam Book
has been completely reset in a type face
designed for easy reading, and was printed
from new plates. It contains the complete
text of the original hard-cover edition.*
NOT ONE WORD HAS BEEN OMITTED.

RL 6, 009-013

IRISH RED

*A Bantam Book | published by arrangement with
Holiday House, Inc.*

*PRINTING HISTORY*

*Holiday House edition published in 1951*

*Bantam Skylark Edition | February 1977*

| | |
|---|---|
| *2nd printing .... September 1977* | *6th printing ......... June 1980* |
| *3rd printing ..... November 1978* | *7th printing ..... February 1981* |
| *4th printing ......... June 1979* | *8th printing ..... December 1982* |
| *5th printing ........ March 1980* | *9th printing ......... May 1984* |

*Skylark Books is a registered trademark of Bantam Books, Inc.,
Registered in the U.S. Patent Office and elsewhere.*

ISBN 0-553-15286-6

*Published simultaneously in the United States and Canada*

*Bantam Books are published by Bantam Books, Inc. Its trade-
mark, consisting of the words ''Bantam Books'' and the por-
trayal of a rooster, is Registered in U.S. Patent and Trademark
Office and in other countries. Marca Registrada. Bantam
Books, Inc., 666 Fifth Avenue, New York, New York 10103.*

PRINTED IN THE UNITED STATES OF AMERICA

CW    18  17  16  15  14  13  12  11  10

For Dilla Macbean

# Contents

# 1. Muttonhead

Danny Pickett was mad clear through. Gingerly he made his way across the Pickett yard, leaving muddy little puddles to mark his path. Reaching the cabin's porch, he unlaced his muddy shoes, kicked them off, and took off his socks. Stooping to wring out his trouser legs, Danny went into the cabin and slammed the door shut behind him.

He took a folded newspaper from a pile on a shelf, spread it out on the floor, stepped onto the paper, and unbuttoned his soaked shirt. He let it fall on the paper, dropped his trousers beside it, then his underwear.

Danny crossed the floor to the big tin washtub that doubled as the Picketts' bathtub, took a tin basin from the wooden table beside the sink, and pumped it full of water. He emptied it into the tub and filled it again, and again. When the tub was half filled, Danny emptied the contents of the simmering tea-kettle into the tub, and tested the water with his finger. It was tepid.

Muttering to himself, he got a wash cloth and towel and stepped in. Danny washed himself, letting water run out of the wash cloth over his lithe young body and back into the tub. When the worst part of the muck that covered him had been removed, he began to rub himself vigorously with the wash cloth.

There was a tread on the porch, a shadow at the door, and Ross Pickett, Danny's father, came into the room. A pail filled with wild raspberries dangled from his hand, but Ross seemed to forget them while he stared incredulously at his son.

"Why you takin' a bath, Danny? It's not Saturday, and right in midday like this. You feel poorly?"

"Gah!" Danny stepped out of the tub onto the floor and began to rub himself with the towel. "Sometimes I wonder if I was right about Irish setters!"

"What you mean?"

"That Mike pup, he's got about as many brains as a half-witted jack rabbit!"

"What's Mike done?"

"The pig pen," Danny moaned. "He got in the pig pen and started chasing the pigs around! And when I called him he waded into the hog wallow! Right up to his neck he went, and stood there barking at me! When I made a grab for his collar, he jumped back and I fell into the wallow!"

Ross tittered, but stopped when Danny glared at him.

"What'd you do then?" Ross grinned.

"What could I do? He stuck his hind end up in the air, got down on his front quarters, and barked some more. Thought I wanted to play. Then he took off after a blue jay. I don't know where he went. And I don't care."

"He won't go far," Ross said. He put down his pail. "I came by the big house, Danny. Thought Mr. Haggin would like some wild berries."

"Anything new down there?"

"Yeah." Ross frowned. "Mr. Haggin's goin' away. He's leavin' the big place in care of his nephew, a fancy-pants by the name of John Price. Givin' him a mighty free hand with everything, he is."

"A boss should have a free hand, shouldn't he?"

"Maybe so, but this John Price, he don't like Irish setters at all."

"No!" Danny said, astounded.

Ross grunted. " 'So you're Ross Pickett,' he says to me, 'one of Uncle Dick's Irish setter men? Well, there are some dogs that can beat the red pants right off your Irishmen and I've got 'em right here.' Then he took me over to some little fences he had built, kennels, he called 'em, and showed me some black and white dogs. English setters, he called 'em."

"How did they look?"

"They are," Ross said reluctantly, "a right smart lot of dog. There's even a trainer for 'em, man named Joe Williams. Danny, there's trouble afoot."

"We've had trouble before, Pappy."

"If it comes," Ross predicted, "this'll be a different kind. Well, no use killin' your bears before you see 'em. I'll go find Mike."

Danny, no longer angry, worried a bit as he got into clean clothes. To him, Irish setters were far and away the world's best dogs, but it was not unthinkable that other people had their favorites too. It was hard to imagine Mr. Haggin putting Irish setters aside in favor of anything else. Danny thought back over the chain of events that had led to this new development.

It all started when Mr. Haggin, a wealthy industrialist who had built an estate in the wild Wintapi region, bought Big Red, a champion Irish setter. When Red and Danny met, it was a case of mutual love at first sight and the big setter had refused to leave the boy. Mr. Haggin, with visions of producing the world's finest strain of Irish setters, had hired Danny to take care of Red and later had bought Sheilah MacGuire, another champion, as a mate for Red.

At first, Ross, strictly a hound man, had been scornful of the setters. Then Old Majesty, the Wintapi's huge outlaw bear, had killed Ross's hounds and hurt Ross himself. Danny and Red had brought Old Majesty to bay and killed him, but in so doing, Red was permanently injured. He was forever spoiled for shows, and Danny had bought him from Mr. Haggin.

Then Sheilah had become the mother of five pups. Mr. Haggin was delighted because four of them were certain show material and would surely be able to hold their own with the best. Ross, who had given his whole heart to Irish setters when he finally admitted their worth, doted on Mike, the fifth pup, who was a runt, misfit, trouble-maker, and general all-around muddle-head.

That was strange because Ross had an eye for any sort of animal, and could determine quality almost at a glance. Even a casual observer could tell that any of Mike's three sisters, or his brother, were far superior. At five months of age, their worth showed plainly. But Mike. . . .

Fairly well-built, he was nevertheless too small and too narrow in the back ever to take a championship, or even a third place. And what he had in his head seemed to consist almost exclusively of an immense talent for mischief. Danny had a sudden disquieting thought. Was Mr. Haggin angry because Sheilah had thrown a runt? Then he shrugged and forgot it. Mr. Haggin would not get rid of his Irish setters, nor would he let anyone else do so. Ross worried about nothing.

There was a startled squawk, followed by a continuous outraged squalling. Danny ran to the door.

Still crusted with dried mud from the hog wallow, and having abandoned hope of catching the blue jay, Mike had returned to the Pickett yard. Pussyfooting, he had crawled up on Ross's speckled rooster until he was within springing distance. Then he had lunged and grabbed the bird by its tail. Now he hung on, straining backward while the hysterical rooster flapped its wings and sought an escape. Danny opened the door.

"Hey! You, Mike!"

The puppy braced his feet a little more firmly, jerked, and snapped the struggling rooster backward. Danny started toward him, but just then Ross came around a corner of the wood shed. Danny stopped to await developments.

Kneeling, Ross caught the puppy, gently disengaged his jaws, and the still-squawking rooster scuttled away. Danny's jaw drooped sarcastically as he heard his father's voice.

"Bad. Bad dog."

The puppy wriggled into Ross's arms, and bent his head back. He started licking Ross's face with a warm, sticky tongue, and Danny's father raised a hand to shield himself. Danny stole up behind them.

"You two having a real confidential talk?"

"Stop it!" Ross sputtered. "Cut it out, Mike!"

Ross rose. Released, the puppy started galloping full speed around the pair and barking at the top of his voice. He stopped suddenly, front quarters close to the ground and rear ones thrust straight up in the air. His tail wagged furiously as he continued to bark. Then he dashed at Ross and began a ferocious attack on his shoelaces. Ross looked down.

"A right peppery pup," he announced. "Just full of hell and high water. But he'll get over it."

Danny glanced toward the chastened rooster, who had run to the pig pen and now lingered near it, ready to dash underneath.

"Hope we got some chickens left by that time," he said dryly. "You should have hided him for tackling the rooster."

"And who," Ross scoffed, "has been tellin' me you can't lick Irish setters if you ever expect to get anywhere with 'em?"

"Red never needed any lickings," Danny defended. "But I don't know what else you can do to a pup with as little sense as this one."

"Mike's goin' to come around when he does a little more growin'. No pup's got sense."

"Sean has. So have Eileen, Sharon, and Pat."

"Sean's somethin' besides just a dog. He's got a lot of both Red and Sheilah in him. But Mike has somethin' Sean lacks."

"Just what is that?"

"Somethin' I can't rightly name," Ross admitted. "But I've seen it before this in more than one animal. He'll show it plain when he forgets his nonsense."

"He's sure got a lot of forgetting to do. Let's put him back in his cage."

The puppy gamboled at their heels when they started back toward the wire cage Danny had built to hold all five pups. The other four leaped against the wire and welcomed them with a barking chorus when they came near, then pushed their heads against the wire to have their ears scratched. Danny stooped to gather Mike in his arms, and lifted him over the wire. Mike reared, waving his front paws, then began to tussle with one of his sisters.

Danny stared, mystified, at the enclosure. It was four feet high, built of sturdy, galvanized mesh and supported by solid posts. Aware of a puppy's propensity for digging, Danny had buried the bottom eighteen inches of the wire. He looked wonderingly at Mike.

There were no holes through the wire or under it, and the gate remained firmly locked. Danny scratched his head. There was no possible way for one of the pups to get out, but Mike had escaped. Danny looked at Ross.

"How the dickens does he get out?"

"Search me, Danny."

"Must have slipped through the gate after I fed 'em this morning. Well, he's in now."

They leaned on the fence, gazing admiringly at the pups. Danny was aware of motion beside him, and a velvet-soft muzzle was thrust into his hand. He looked down at the gentle Sheilah, mother of the five pups, and closed his fingers around her muzzle.

Sheilah had endured the trying ordeals of motherhood without ruffling one of her silken hairs. She had fed her pups, watched over them tenderly, and punished them when they needed it. But now that the pups were weaned, and fenced, Sheilah was treating herself to a well-deserved vacation. She sprawled on the porch, or took long walks with Danny and Ross, except when one of her own children got outside their fence. Then Sheilah was nowhere to be found.

She wagged an apologetic tail, left Danny, and went over to receive her share of petting from Ross. Danny watched from the corner of his eye. From the very first, Sheilah had been more Ross's dog than Danny's. But that was only natural; Sheilah understood the unbreakable bonds existing between Danny and Red, and she could not wriggle inside those bonds. Danny liked Sheilah, but he loved Big Red.

Sheilah padded quietly behind them as they walked back to the cabin, and when Ross went in, Sheilah accompanied him. Danny remained where he was. Red, even more anxious than Sheilah to stay out of the puppies' way, had disappeared early this morning. Danny put his fingers in his mouth, whistled shrilly, and sat down to await results.

Two minutes later his eye was attracted by motion within the beeches that rimmed the Pickett clearing. Danny kept his eyes on it. A second later Red broke out of the trees and started toward the cabin.

Danny watched, pleased with what he saw but smiling a little wistfully. A few months ago Red had been perfection itself, incapable of graceless action. That was before he'd been hurt in the great fight with Old Majesty. Red would always carry evidence of that fight, for now he walked and ran with a pronounced limp. But he was still, Danny thought, the finest dog in the world.

He came up on the porch and sat beside Danny, swinging his great head over his young master's shoulder. Danny tickled his soft ear.

"You, Red," he murmured. "You old bum. For a dog like you, you sure can throw some half-witted sons."

Red muzzled Danny affectionately, and Danny tickled his other ear. Then he rose and walked down the steps. Red padded contentedly beside him as Danny struck the Stoney Lonesome trail.

There were plenty of things to think about, and he could always think more clearly in the woods. Red wandered to one side to nose through a thicket of little hemlocks that had found a rooting among the beeches. Absently Danny watched him.

Until Red came along, Danny had never thought much about his future because, unless you wanted to leave, which he didn't, there was only one future in the beech woods. You took your living from the country, trapping, hunting, guiding hunters and fishermen, and doing whatever odd jobs you could get. Ross had lived in such a fashion all his life, and Danny had fully intended to do the same because, of all the places he could think of, none was as nice as the Wintapi.

Danny had always dreamed of a dog, a great and wonderful dog to be his staunch friend and constant companion, and that dog had materialized in Red. Then the rest of it had happened almost miraculously and opened new vistas of which, previously, Danny had not even dreamed.

There could be, Danny thought, no finer career than rearing and training fine dogs. If a man liked that work well enough, and had the chance, he'd do it without pay. But Mr. Haggin was paying Danny, and Danny felt keenly the additional responsibilities which that placed upon him.

He must be certain that he was working in the right direction. As far as the right direction for Mike was concerned, wouldn't the reckless puppy and everyone else be better off if he were given away to serve as somebody's pet? Regardless of a dog's other qualities, he was of no practical value unless he was intelligent too.

Nothing sensible ever seemed to penetrate Mike's skull. He did what he wished when he wanted to do it, and defied the consequences. Mike had escaped death by a narrow margin a half dozen times, but he never hesitated to gallop headlong into new adventures, and it never seemed to occur to him even to think of what he was doing.

Still, Ross's judgment was sound most of the time. He thought Mike was just a pup who in time would outgrow his silly and bull-headed ideas. Well, only time could tell and Danny would hope for the best. Somehow, Mike might amount to something.

Coming to a steep, aspen-bordered pitch, Danny climbed more slowly. He looked ahead, where Red was loping swiftly up the trail, intent on something he saw, heard, or smelled. Then, between the bordering aspens, he snapped to a dead stop. His head swung, then froze in position. Plumed tail was stiff behind him. One fore paw curled. Danny stopped, watching the scene in sheer delight.

He knew that Red was on a ruffed grouse, a partridge, and since the hens with half-grown broods would not be likely to frequent a trail, doubtless Red had found a wise old cock bird. He stood exactly where he was, holding perfectly.

Then there was an excited rush. Danny caught glimpses of a flying red ball that resolved itself into another dog, and Mike galloped past. Tail wagging hysterically, he dashed past his father straight at the partridge. There was a rattle of wings as the partridge rose and Danny caught fleeting glimpses as it winged through the aspens.

Danny shook a disgusted head. Of course nobody could expect a puppy to point and hold a partridge, or even to honor a point. But any normal pup, coming upon his master, would have stopped. Danny walked impatiently forward.

Red turned in the trail, stiff-legged and stiff-tailed, and a warning growl rumbled from his chest. Mike galloped out of the woods, paying no attention to his father's rumbled warnings, and wagged happily up. Danny hurried. He did not think Red would hurt the puppy, but Mike was enough to try a saint's patience and Red might decide to snap at him. Danny came nearer, then stopped abruptly.

"You, Mike!" he cried. "You muttonhead!"

A dozen white-tipped porcupine quills were imbedded in the puppy's upper jaw. Obviously, coming up the trail, he had discovered and enthusiastically attacked some grunting old porcupine. Now he stood looking up at his master, and though Danny knew that he must be in pain, his tail was wagging and his eyes were glowing. Even a face full of porcupine quills could not ruin the pleasure Mike had found in a forbidden run through the woods. Danny's heart melted.

"Poor pup," he soothed. "Poor little Mike! You would have to meet your first porky while you're so little, and all alone!"

Danny turned back down the trail, and Red hurried to get far enough ahead so he would not be near his son. Mike, beginning to feel the effect of the porcupine's spears, fell in beside Danny. But when Danny tried to pick him up, Mike would have none of it. Danny let him walk. Mike could hardly be blamed for tackling a porcupine. Most puppies, meeting one of the clumsy, spiny beasts for the first time, could not resist getting too near.

Mike pricked his ears up, galloped ahead of

Danny, and made a right-angle turn from the trail. Danny began to run, suspecting that the porcupine was the cause of Mike's excitement. He heard the pup barking furiously, and found him leaping against a birch tree. A big quill pig crouched half-way to the top; Mike's attack must have been furious. Danny turned to Mike.

"Come on, you little fool. Figure you need some more quills?"

Danny's misgivings returned full force. Most dogs would fight a porcupine once. Few were silly enough to try it a second time, and not within a half hour after the first. Danny shook his head in despair.

When he entered the clearing, Red was on the porch and Ross was working on the wood pile. Ross looked up.

"What happened?"

"Tangled with a porcupine."

"Poor little cuss," Ross soothed. "I'll get the neatsfoot and a pair of pliers."

Danny knelt to pass his arms around the squirm-ing puppy while Ross worked neatsfoot oil around the base of each quill. The puppy shivered with pain, but made no outcry.

"Nothin' wrong with his heart," Ross announced.

Ross grasped a quill with his pliers, and quickly jerked it out. As the puppy tried to break away, Danny took a firmer grip. It was not a job he liked, but it was one that had to be done. Ross worked as swiftly and as humanely as he could while Danny held Mike. Finally Ross got up, the last quill still clenched in his pliers.

"There," he announced, as he brushed the perspiration from his forehead. "Guess you learned somethin' today, Mike."

Mike wriggled his tail, sat down, and began to soothe the many aches in his jaw with a soft tongue. Suddenly Red growled, and Danny and Ross swung to see two horsemen coming up the trail from the Haggin estate. One was Mr. Haggin himself. Danny had never seen the other.

"That's John Price," Ross said, "and he's got one of them new dogs with him."

Danny's eyes centered on the dog, a beautiful English setter that stayed far enough from the horses so they would not run him down. Danny stared in admiration. It was a fine dog, a gorgeous creature that somehow reminded him of Red in manner and bearing. Quality was stamped all over him.

The horsemen came near the cabin, and at a soft word of command the dog sat down. He was young, but obviously had been well trained.

Mr. Haggin spoke from the saddle. "I'm glad to find you home, Danny. I want you to meet my nephew, John Price. He'll be taking over while I'm away and—"

He was interrupted by a throaty growl from Mike. The red puppy sprang from the porch to land squarely on top of the young English setter. Immediately they were tumbling in a dog fight.

# 2. Irish or English?

Attacking first, Mike won the advantage of surprise and used it to good advantage. The red puppy snapped half a dozen times before the other dog could bring himself to retaliate.

Something registered in Danny's brain. The English setter was a wonderful dog, but something was missing. It was not that he lacked the courage to defend himself; lack of initiative seemed to be his trouble. He had, Danny thought, been cast in too rigid a mold. Doubtless he would respond perfectly and immediately to any command of his trainer, and probably, as he grew older, he would be a superb hunter. But he was like a man who cannot think for himself, who must always look to a superior before he can act. When an unexpected situation arose, the English setter did not know how to meet it.

Never at a loss no matter what happened, Mike dodged away when the English setter finally struggled to his feet. Mike came in to strike at his enemy's flank and was away, whirling and twisting on dancing paws which, for all their puppy clumsiness, did exactly what he wanted them to do.

Finally becoming oriented, the young English setter snarled in to strike. But Mike had spent too many hours frolicking with his brother and sisters not to know how to roll with a punch. His enemy's teeth snapped only on a mouthful of red fur, and

Mike struck twice while the English setter was preparing a new attack.

Danny shouted a command which he knew Mike would ignore anyway, then jumped from the porch to part the fighting dogs. John Price was there a second sooner.

He slid from his black horse, raised his riding crop, and slashed Mike across the face. He struck again, and was preparing to hit a third time, when Mike backed away.

He did not cringe or slink, as a beaten or spiritless dog would, nor did he display any hostility toward this new and unexpected assailant. For generations Mike's breed had been taught that their place was with men. Only in protection of his own master, or his master's household, would an Irish setter attack a human being.

Mike had no thought of striking back at John Price, but he could take the measure of this man and file it away in his brain for future reference. He backed warily, keeping cautious eyes on the riding crop. Mike dodged aside when the man rushed him, and feinted to the other side when he rushed again. Both times the riding crop slashed only empty air.

Then Danny was between Mike and his attacker. Danny's sinewy fingers closed and tightened about the hand that held the riding crop.

"Stop it!" he commanded.

For a moment they stood eye to eye, two young men who took each other's measure much as Mike had taken John Price's. When the other tried to jerk away, Danny tightened his fingers. Then John Price relaxed and Danny let him go. Grimly he stepped back.

"No need to keep on hitting a dog after he's stopped fighting."

"He could use a lesson!"

"He don't get his lessons with whips!"

Mr. Haggin had dismounted and was holding the young English setter's collar. Turning his back on Danny, John Price walked back to the black and white dog. He stooped, and explored with probing fingers. Then he rose.

"He isn't hurt," he said to Mr. Haggin.

"I wouldn't think so." Mr. Haggin sounded slightly sarcastic. "That puppy isn't more than five months old."

Ross had caught Mike, and now stood uncertainly near. This was not the way things should have happened. But they had happened, and he would stand by Danny and Mike.

"Little pepper pot," Mr. Haggin grinned, coming toward them. "Wonder what possessed him?"

"No telling what possesses Mike to do anything," Danny said. "Guess he just wanted a fight."

"As I was saying when I was so rudely interrupted," Mr. Haggin continued, "I thought it would be a good idea if you met my nephew. John, shake hands with Danny Pickett."

John Price spoke to the English setter, who dropped instantly, and came forward. He had, Danny decided, been annoyed when Mike jumped his dog. Well, that might make anybody mad and John Price seemed over it now. He smiled and extended his hand.

"Glad to know you, Danny."

"And I'm glad to know you."

Mr. Haggin took over. "I'm going on a rather extended trip, guess you both know that? I've been awaiting the opportunity a long while, but until I got hold of John I didn't have anybody to leave in command here. I just want both of you to know that John will be in complete charge, and you can go to him for anything you need."

"We'll get along," Ross said.

"I'm sure you will."

"Where are you going, Mr. Haggin?" Danny inquired.

"Quite a few places, Danny. I'm going to look at some of the world's best horses, cattle, and sheep, and see if I can bring back anything that will improve our Wintapi stock. I'll be in Arabia, Holland, England, Ireland, and maybe other countries." Mischief lighted his eyes. "Maybe I'll even find a better Irishman than Big Red."

"There aren't any!" Danny said quickly.

John Price laughed, then gestured toward Mike with his riding crop.

"You told me you had champion Irish setters up here, Uncle Dick. Do you call that one?"

"Mike's one of Sheilah's pups, but I admit he isn't much like his father or mother."

"Where are the rest of them?"

Ross spoke up, "Red and Sheilah's prowlin' some-where. The rest of the pups are penned."

John Price looked puzzled. "You let prize-win-ning dogs roam at will?"

Ross shrugged. "Why not? Irish setters was meant to run loose. You can't keep 'em in any piddlin' little coop and make 'em like it."

John Price gave him a sharp look.

"May I see the pups?"

"Sure," said Ross, retaining his hold on Mike.

When they started away, the black and white setter half rose. John Price spoke sharply and the dog settled back down on the grass. Danny frowned, not understanding. A dog was more than just an ani-mal. He furnished love, and loyalty, and com-panionship, and something that made you feel warm inside when you and your dog were all alone in the deep woods. A dog was not merely something that dropped, or heeled, or fetched, on command, as though he were always in a cage fashioned of his master's thought and will. Plainly John Price thought of dogs in a way that had never occurred to either Danny or Ross.

Danny fell in beside Mr. Haggin, and they fol-lowed Ross and John Price toward the wire cage. Sheilah's four children came yelling to meet them, and reared against the wire. Ross picked Mike up and dropped him beside his brother and sisters.

"Ever see a nicer-looking bunch of pups?" Mr. Haggin said proudly.

For a moment John Price did not speak. "No," he

said slowly, "I never did, Uncle Dick. I never saw a nicer-looking bunch—or a more useless one."

"Useless?" Danny bristled.

"That's exactly what I mean. What are those four pups ever going to do besides add to Uncle Dick's collection of blue ribbons? The fifth won't even do that; he might better be shot right now."

"Shot!" Danny gasped.

"It's straight talk. Oh, nobody will deny that the Irishman's a beautiful dog; the average Irish setter has a more striking appearance and more flash than bench winners of almost any other breed. That's exactly their trouble. People who care more about looks than anything else have taken the Irishmen over; everything except an ability to win blue ribbons at dog shows has been bred out of them."

"Did you ever shoot behind a good Irish setter?"

John Price laughed. "There aren't any good ones."

"That isn't so! My Red dog, he'll outrun and out-hunt anything that's ever been in the Wintapi!"

Danny stopped, remembering something he had momentarily forgotten. Red *had* been able to outrun and out-hunt anything in the Wintapi. Red was now a cripple. His hunting ability was unimpaired, but he couldn't possibly match the pace of a young, fast dog.

"Before you two get to fighting," Mr. Haggin said, "maybe I'd better explain what this is all about. John's got the idea that, if we switch to English setters, we can collect some field trial cups as well as bench wins. He says he'll prove it. The dog that

came up here with us, John says, is going to take the
National Field Trials."

"You," Danny stammered, "you aren't going to
sell your Irish setters?"

"Not yet anyhow; John hasn't proven a thing. But
I'll back the best dog."

"Oh," Danny said.

He felt a dull emptiness that began at the pit of
his stomach and spread both ways. Until now, there
had been no word or thought of selling Sheilah
and the pups, and switching to some other dog.
Danny was staggered by the very thought of such a
thing. John Price spoke eagerly.

"Let me show you what I mean, Uncle Dick! Obviously these pups haven't even been yard-broken,
but you said there were two older dogs here and
both hunted. Pit either of them against any of the
eight English setters I brought, and you'll see the
difference yourself!"

Mr. Haggin looked at Danny. "What do you say?"

Danny shook a miserable head. "Red couldn't
keep up in a fast heat. You know that."

"Sheilah hunts."

"You have to understand Sheilah, Mr. Haggin.
She'll hunt for us, but I don't know what she'd show
if you put her down and made her hunt."

John Price was grinning triumphantly. Ross
noticed it.

"We'll bring Sheilah down," he said. "When?"

"Tomorrow morning at eight," John Price said.

"We'll be there."

The two men remounted their horses, and on

command the black and white English setter rose to follow. Danny stared at their retreating backs, and turned to Ross.

"Why did you say that?"

"That John Price, he thought we were afraid."

"You know Sheilah."

"We can't back down, Danny."

"Better rub your rabbit's foot, then. We'll need all the luck we can get."

Danny strolled gloomily to the cabin. Red was nowhere to be seen, but Sheilah, who had taken herself elsewhere while strangers visited, thumped the floor boards with her plumed tail as Danny approached. Danny stooped to stroke her head.

Never a fast or flashy hunter, or one that cared a bit about playing to the grandstand, Sheilah was still a first-rate gun dog and able to hold her own in most company. Trouble would arise because of her make-up.

She was so gentle, and emotional, that a harsh word could send her trembling into the nearest corner. At all times she must be positive that she was in the good graces of the human beings around her, but so well had Danny and Ross handled her that, in turn, Sheilah gave herself completely to them. She trusted no one else, and regardless of how they coaxed, she would never let herself be caressed by anyone else. She was strictly a one-family dog who would break her heart for the people she loved and trusted. What would she do if other people were present and how would she react when competing with one of John Price's robots? Tomorrow would tell that tale.

Red limped out of the woods onto the porch, threw himself down beside Sheilah, and Danny scratched the big dog's ears. A lump rose in his throat. There had been a time, not too long ago, when Red could have challenged anything in John Price's kennels and beaten it easily. That time was past and would never come back again. Danny sighed and got up; it was time to give the pups a run.

He let Red and Sheilah into the cabin and opened the gate to the puppies' cage. Out they boiled, streaming past Danny as they raced helter-skelter across the clearing. The gorgeous Sean, perfection itself, led the pack. Then came his three sisters while, for a moment, Mike lagged in the rear.

Danny's eyes widened. Mike was the smallest of the pups, and therefore the shortest-legged. But Mike never had been one to let minor handicaps interfere with the more important things and right now the most important consisted of catching Sean. Mike lengthened out, his belly seeming to scrape the ground as his pace became swifter. Plumed tail fluttered straight behind him, and his slim body undulated. A happy grin framed his face.

Almost without effort he passed his three sisters and bore down on Sean. The lead puppy glanced back over his shoulder and accepted the challenge. Like ground-skimming birds they flew to the far end of the clearing, and it was there that Mike finally caught his swift brother. Instantly he attacked, and the two puppies rolled in another of their endless mock fights.

Danny watched, puzzled and interested. Sean had been doing his best, but Mike had caught him. The smallest of the litter, he was also the fastest. And certainly there was nothing wrong with his courage. Two minutes after Ross had finished pulling porcupine quills out of his face, he had jumped headlong into a fight with a bigger, heavier dog. Danny shook his head.

Mike was fast and courageous, but he was also bull-headed. Always wanting his own way, he never gave an inch to anything that might stand in his path. He would be worthless unless he developed some brains and showed some willingness to cooperate.

Two hours later, shortly before dark, the panting puppy pack returned. All were soaking wet, they had been swimming in the creek, and in addition Mike had a torn ear. Somewhere out in the beech woods he had run into something, probably a prowling coon, and had evidently tried to start another fight with it.

Danny locked all five puppies in the barn, and gave them a huge pan full of food, which they started gobbling instantly. Mike, always alert for the main chance, climbed into the middle of the pan and calmly proceeded to usurp the lion's share. Danny grinned. By any reasonable rules Mike should have been the biggest dog in the pack; he ate half again as much as any of his companions.

Soberly Danny strolled into the cabin. Red rose

to come greet him, but the more restrained Sheilah wagged her welcome from the carpet in the middle of the floor. Red sat beside him when Danny seated himself on a chair and stared thoughtfully at Sheilah.

"If your face gets any longer, your lower jaw will be hittin' your knees," Ross observed from the stove. "What's the matter, Danny?"

"Nothing."

"Yes, there is. You're afraid of tomorrow mornin', huh?"

"We shouldn't be using Sheilah."

Hearing her name, Sheilah rose and padded over to sit quietly at Danny's other side. Danny stroked her sleek head.

"Sheilah's a good hunter," Ross said.

"Sure. I know it and you know it. But is she going to prove it for Mr. Haggin and his nephew?"

Ross said quietly, "Danny, why did you take up with these Irish setters?"

"Because I believe in them."

"Then don't let Sheilah down by lickin' her yourself, before Haggin's dog does it."

"Suppose he does it?"

"He ain't done it yet. Set the table."

Danny spent a restless night, and pecked at the breakfast Ross cooked. He locked Sean and his three sisters in the wire cage, led the unwilling Mike into the cabin, and shut the door. At once Mike reared with his paws on the window sill, his face plastered against the window. Mike entreated Danny with pleading eyes and wagging tail, and when Danny refused to let him out he set up a howling that could be heard a quarter of a mile away.

"Let him screech," Ross said. "He won't bother anythin', except maybe a squirrel or two."

When Ross snapped his fingers, Sheilah trotted confidently over to walk beside him. Danny fell in with the pair, and when Red would have followed Danny ordered him back. Red sat down in the path, ears flattened and eyes disconsolate as he watched the trio enter the woods. In Red's opinion it was not right for Danny to go anywhere unless he went along, but he made no attempt to follow.

Without speaking they strode down the Smokey Creek trail, crossed the bridge, and came to the edge of the extensive Haggin estate. Ross worked his lips, as though he was about to say something, but he did not speak. Danny glanced sideways, knowing that his father was tense, too.

As they approached the big barns, Sheilah slowed her step and walked so close to Ross that she all but brushed his legs. Curley Jordan, one of Mr. Haggin's men and a good friend of the Picketts, was exercising a stallion in the yard. He jerked a calloused thumb toward the house.

"Boss said to tell you he won't be long. Stick around."

They sat down in the grass, Sheilah resting companionably between the two, and watched Curley work. Then a stranger, dressed in jodhpurs and leather leggings, emerged from one of the tenant houses and came toward them.

He was a tall man with a fading thatch of brown

hair. His face, sun-tanned and wind-creased, had obviously been exposed to every sort of weather. He smiled as he came forward.

"So you're my competition, are you?"

"Guess so," Danny said. "Would you be John Price's trainer?"

"That's me, Joe Williams."

He looked keenly at Sheilah, and Danny warmed to him. His was the air of a man who knew dogs, and plainly he was able to see Sheilah's good points as well as her few flaws. When he came near, Sheilah pressed her sleek head tightly against Ross's shoulder and refused to look around.

"She doesn't take kindly to anybody she doesn't know," Danny explained.

"I understand. Is she the best you've got?"

"Not the best hunter, but we can't run him; he's crippled. All we've got except Sheilah and Red are five unbroken pups."

"Uh-huh. Would it be fair enough if you ran her against another bitch her own age?"

"Sure," Ross said.

"I'll get Belle."

Joe Williams disappeared behind the barn, and reappeared in a short time with another English setter beside him. Danny whistled his admiration. If John Price had personally selected these English setters, he knew good stock. Belle was like the young dog that Mike had fought, but more finished. There was fire in her, and quality, and plenty of breeding. Still. . . . Danny wrinkled his brow.

There was something else about John Price's

dogs, something Danny could not understand at all. Belle was not on a leash, but she still seemed to be confined, as though her trainer were the source of all power and strength. There could be no doubt that the English setters were perfectly trained, but they seemed to lack spontaneity. At the moment Danny could not decide whether that was good or bad.

A few minutes later John Price and Mr. Haggin appeared.

"All set, I see," Mr. Haggin said. "Good. The heats will be run in the back field. Of course they won't be formal, and we'll sort of figure out the rules as we go along. All right?"

Danny walked with the group, but because Sheilah did not like to be so close to strangers, Ross dropped back. They crossed Mr. Haggin's broad meadows, went through a straggling line of woods, and came into one of the uncultivated back fields. Danny looked questioningly at a wooden crate beneath a tree, and Mr. Haggin saw his glance.

"John wanted to be sure there'd be birds to find, so we had some pheasants brought up."

"I see."

Danny kept his own counsel, not voicing the protest that sprang to his lips. As far as he knew, Sheilah had never worked on anything except grouse and quail. Pheasants were entirely different, but they were game birds and Mr. Haggin was certainly trying to be fair. The heats could have been run under very formal rules, and if either dog did not live up to them, disqualification would be the penalty.

Knowing that neither Danny nor Ross had ever taken part in such a trial, Mr. Haggin had said that the rules would be made as they went along. Sheilah had a chance.

John Price took over. "Each handler will start his dog at this corner of the field and make a complete circuit. We'll plant one bird for each, and the winner will be the dog that holds and points best. Any objections?"

Ross shrugged his acceptance. Danny said nothing.

"Do you want to go first?" Price asked Ross.

"Nope, let Joe lead off."

Danny relaxed. He had been wondering just what a handler did, and how he acted, in a trial such as this. Ross had solved that neatly by accepting second place; he could watch Joe Williams and do whatever he did.

"I'll plant your bird, Joe," John Price said.

He walked down to the crate, cautiously opened the trap door, reached in, brought out a struggling hen pheasant, and folded his hands about both wings. He whirled the pheasant around a few times, tucked its head under one wing, and put it down in a bunch of tall grass.

Danny approved; evidently John Price knew a lot about both dogs and birds. A pheasant, treated in such a manner, was hypnotized and would remain quiet for a considerable time.

"All right, Joe," Price called.

Joe Williams moved away with the English setter beside him. He spoke some command, some word that Danny could not hear, and the dog started to hunt. Danny kept his eyes on her.

A beautiful creature, she seemed to acquire added beauty and grace now that she was hunting. All fire and flesh, she raced so swiftly that her trainer began to run to keep up. But at another command the dog slowed slightly. Danny narrowed his eyes.

There still seemed to be an invisible leash stretching from Belle to her trainer. They worked together in almost perfect coordination, and that was good. There was still something about it that he didn't like.

Certainly Belle was a superb hunter, and she was enjoying the hunt, but not to the same extent that Red would. He threw himself heart and soul into the game, and worked as perfectly with Danny as Belle was working with Joe Williams, from sheer love of hunting and for Danny. Belle seemed a little strained, a little mechanical, as though she could never forget there was a man behind her. She was a wonderful hunter. Red was an artistic one.

Danny's eyes were attracted by motion at the far end of the field. He saw two grouse come out of the beech woods into the open meadow, and disappear in tall grass. Probably they were looking for seeds, or had a dust bath in the grass. Danny's eyes returned to the dog.

She was almost at the far end of the field, turning to come back toward her planted game. When they neared the pheasant, Joe Williams dropped a little behind his dog. He was not going to make the mistake of pointing it out to her.

Nor did he have to. Getting bird scent, Belle stopped instantly. She froze in a point, plumed tail stiff and one fore paw lifted. Joe Williams edged up to flush the pheasant.

It flew so close to the grass tops that its beating wings sent little air currents ruffling through them. Joe Williams called his dog to heel and came in.

Danny gulped. It had been a wonderful performance, almost a perfect one. Before he was hurt Red could have done as well or better, but Danny looked doubtfully at Sheilah.

John Price planted another bird and called, "All right, Ross."

Sheilah crowded close beside Ross as he started off, following the path laid out by Joe Williams. Danny crossed his fingers and breathed hard; this was exactly what he had feared. Sheilah, upset by close contact with too many strangers, had no intention of leaving Ross's side. Besides Danny, only Joe Williams seemed to know that.

"That's a good dog," the trainer said, "but she's strictly one-man. Right now she's nervous as a hurt cat."

"Yes, darn it," Danny agreed.

They were in the far corner of the field before Sheilah would hunt at all. Then she trotted forward, casting as a hunting dog will, and Danny's heart sang. Sheilah lacked Belle's ability to impress an audience. But she was hunting almost as well and there was something present here that had been absent from Belle's performance—something free and easy.

Never since Danny and Ross had had her had Sheilah known a whipping or even a slap. Never had she been forced to do anything which love for Danny and Ross would not have made her do anyway. It showed in the way she hunted. Danny's eyes glowed. This was the way a dog should hunt. An Irish setter with Belle's speed, hunting the way Sheilah hunted, would be perfection itself.

They swung to come up, following almost exactly the path laid out by Joe Williams and Belle. Sheilah stopped suddenly.

Danny's heart leaped. The English setter passed within a few feet of where Sheilah was standing, but Belle had missed entirely the two grouse in the field. Sheilah was on them! She edged up and snapped into a perfect point.

Ross walked in ahead of her, and Danny felt suddenly cold. No birds flushed. Nothing at all happened. The two grouse had come into the meadow because they thought themselves perfectly safe. Finding a dog upon them, and too wise to fly, they must have run through the grass and back into the woods.

Danny remembered too late that nobody except himself had seen them come there.

# 3. A New Job

Danny worked on the wood pile furiously, trying by hard labor to forget the worries that beset him. To all eyes except his, Sheilah had taken a bad beating when she ran against John Price's black and white dog. Danny knew that she had not; Sheilah wasn't as fast but she had a better nose. Point for point, she was at least as good as Belle.

Only how could he prove it? Nobody except Danny had seen the grouse come into the field, and at the time he hadn't thought them worth mentioning. To bring it up afterwards, to say that Sheilah had been on birds which the English setter had passed, would sound like the lamest of alibis.

Danny laid a length of tough oak in his chopping block, swung his axe, and split the wood cleanly. He split the two halves to stove size and threw them on the great heap of wood already split. But in spite of furious labor he could not forget his troubles.

Mr. Haggin hadn't said outright that he was going to sell his Irish setters, but neither had he said that he wouldn't. Patting Danny on the shoulder, he had told him to go back up to the cabin and watch over the dogs. That was all and it wasn't enough.

The uncertainty had hung fire long enough, and it wasn't going to hang any longer. Mr. Haggin must say what he intended to do about Sheilah and the pups.

Danny sank his double-bitted axe into the chopping block so hard that he left the handle quivering, and glanced toward the puppies' cage. All five sprawled in the sun; for once even Mike had not escaped. Sheilah had gone bee-hunting with Ross. Whistling for Red, Danny turned toward the Smokey Creek trail.

Red, who had been resting on the porch, arose and quartered out to intercept Danny. The big dog fell in beside him. Danny let his dangling fingers play around Red's ears, and at once he felt better. There was nothing he couldn't do, and no problem he couldn't solve, as long as he kept his self-confidence—and Red. Red raised a moist tongue to lick Danny's hand. Danny smiled. Nobody could feel badly for long if he had a dog like Red beside him.

Side by side, they passed the barns and went to the big house. Red, who had been here so often that he knew exactly what to do, lay down in a sunny corner of the porch. Danny punched the bell, and Mr. Haggin himself opened the door.

"Good morning, Mr. Haggin. Figured I'd better come down and have a talk with you."

"Glad you did, it saved me a trip up to see you. Had breakfast?"

"At sun-up. Pappy wanted to go bee-hunting."

"Um-m! Hope he remembers me with some wild honey; I won't have many more opportunities to enjoy it. I'm leaving tomorrow. Have a cup of coffee anyhow, Danny."

Without waiting for an answer, Mr. Haggin ordered coffee for both of them. Then he looked keenly at him.

"How far wide of the mark would I be if I guessed that you'd come to me about Irish setters?"

"You'd be right on the point ar l holding true," Danny said. "That's just why I'm here."

"What's on your mind, specifically?"

"I'd like to know where Pappy and I stand."

"Where you always did, Danny. I've never in my life hired a man unless I really wanted to keep him. You needn't worry about your job."

"How about Sheilah and the pups?"

"I hope you don't think I'd be fool enough to put everything we did into those Irish setters and then let them go because Sheilah couldn't stand up to Belle."

"She could, Mr. Haggin. You've shot behind her."

"I'm not denying that she's a good gun dog, but she doesn't have Belle's caliber. Red has, but of course he's in a class by himself. It'll be a long while before another one like him happens along. As for you, you worry too much."

"I worry too much?"

"That's it. What did I tell you when I asked you to work with my dogs?"

"You said you wanted me to learn all there is to know about them."

"Think you learned that in a year?"

"Nobody could."

"That's right." Mr. Haggin rose to pace the floor.

"Danny, I have a purpose in this Wintapi estate. Fortunately I also have enough money to back my ideas. I've always been interested in animals, and hope to leave them a little better than I found them. If I can do that I'll be satisfied. As far as the dogs are concerned, I chose Irish setters because I liked them and thought they were the best. I still think so. I also like my nephew and am willing to listen to his ideas. We'll give John's setters a fair trial, and if he can show something better than we have, more power to him.

"I want to be fair, Danny, to you as well as to everyone else. You've done an excellent job as far as you've gone, and you and your father have an instinctive knowledge of dogs. I'm lucky to have you. But instinct isn't everything. When you pitted Sheilah against one of the English setters, I did not expect Sheilah to win. I'm surprised that she did as well as she did. Why? These English setters are in the hands of a professional trainer and as far as I know there aren't any better than Joe Williams. He's devoted his life to his job. It would be unreasonable if he did not know much that you do not."

Danny nodded, remembering the way Joe had handled Belle.

"All right. Now there are five pups, four good ones, with Red and Sheilah's blood, which was the best I was able to find. I'm perfectly aware of the fact that dogs vary; there can be a wide difference between litter mates and the best blood lines in the world aren't within themselves proof of quality.

Look at Mike and you'll know what I mean. However, at least one of the four pups should take to
hunting. I don't necessarily expect any champions—I know they're scarce—but I would like to
see one of those four pups trained so he is able to
hold his own with the average bird dog of any other
breed. If I can get one I'm sticking by the Irishmen,
but I'm not saying that we won't keep the English
setters, too.

"I don't expect you and your dad to make that sort
of hunter out of any pup; it would be unfair to expect you to compete with Joe Williams. I would like
to see you become an all-around setter man, one
able to handle any dog anywhere. Danny, how
would you like to move your stock down here and
work closely with Joe?"

"You mean leave the beech woods?"

"I had the idea," Mr. Haggin said wryly, "that this
place of mine was pretty close to the beech woods
too. However, if this is too civilized for you and
Ross, you could continue to live in your beloved
cabin. Just move Sheilah and the pups down here."

Danny was overwhelmed. "Gosh, Mr. Haggin, I
never thought about training the pups that way."

"Start thinking," Mr. Haggin urged. "I'll put Ross
on the payroll too. Within six months, I expect, he'll
be teaching Joe Williams things."

"That isn't what I meant. Mr. Haggin, these Irish
setters aren't like any other dog. You have to understand them or you can't do a thing with them. They
can think for themselves, and lots of times their

thinking is better than yours. They'll follow their own way when they're bound to and nobody can change that."

"Then you and your dad have a job making Joe understand your Irishmen."

"We could try," said Danny doubtfully.

"Good! That's all I ask of you."

"Suppose it doesn't work?"

Mr. Haggin looked puzzled. "In what way?"

"I don't mean the pups," Danny said hastily. They'll stand up and I know it. But suppose we can't convince your nephew and Joe Williams that they will?"

"In that event, I'm sure John will make any necessary adjustments."

"Well, as I've already said, we can try."

"Good," Mr. Haggin extended his hand. "Happy hunting, Danny."

Danny shook the extended hand heartily, and there was warmth in his voice as he bade Mr. Haggin good-bye. But once he and Red were on the way home, he was assailed by many doubts.

They came to the bridge over Smokey Creek, and Danny stood for a while gazing at his own reflection in the clear pool beneath. Red scrambled down the bank, waded breast deep into the cold water, and drank. A shadowy fish darted across the pool, and Red scrambled after it. Danny grinned.

"Come on," he said. "Come on, you old fish hound. Let's go home and tell Pappy."

Danny brightened at the thought of his father.

Mr. Haggin could be right. Ross could tell at a glance just what any animal was going to do and almost what he was thinking, but perhaps even Ross could learn some new things. They came into the clearing and Mike rushed happily to meet them.

Danny sighed; Mike had been up to more of his tricks. A speckled feather clung to the side of his muzzle.

"You, Mike!" Danny scolded. "Gosh darn your red hide!"

Paying no attention, the red puppy sidled enthusiastically up to Red and seized his ear. Red growled a warning. Ignoring it, Mike braced his paws and jerked backward. Red pulled free and trotted toward the cabin, shaking the abused ear. Then a squawking blue jay flew across the clearing and Mike lengthened out to chase it.

As the red puppy disappeared in the beech woods, the speckled rooster came out from beneath the pig pen. He emerged slowly, looking carefully around before he scuttled for the safety of the chicken coop. A once-proud creature, undisputed ruler of his harem, he was now a disconsolate, dishevelled outcast. All his tail feathers were gone. A brown hen busy with some corn pecked savagely at him. The rooster side-stepped and Danny frowned. The former ruler of the flock was not hurt, but Mike would have to be taught to leave chickens alone.

Mike came tearing back across the clearing, intent on some senseless errand of his own. Danny caught the protesting puppy and dropped him into the cage. As soon as his son was safely behind wire, Red came down from the porch.

The pups, interested in everything that went on, gathered at one side of their cage. When Red started toward them, they broke into a yapping chorus of greeting. Danny unlatched the gate and entered the cage.

Getting his face thoroughly licked in the process, and both his ears nipped, Danny stooped to pick up the puppies' big feed and water dishes, then beat a hasty retreat. He latched the gate while all five pups scrambled furiously against it. Danny filled the water dish with clean, fresh water and replaced it. He fed the puppies, left them gobbling their meal, and looked around the yard. His eye fell on the hens.

The Picketts had twenty-nine chickens of all sizes and colors, and it was a tribute to Red and Sheilah's vigilance that they were able to keep any at all in the beech woods. Furred and feathered raiders came at frequent intervals—none of them averse to a chicken dinner. Furthermore, once such pirates became accustomed to easy meals, they came again and again. The only way to stop them was to kill them.

Danny had been missing one chicken, a yellow game hen, for some time. It did not necessarily follow that she had made a varmint's dinner; game chickens had a liking for the woods and, even though it was late in the season for a hen to feel broody, this one might have stolen her nest somewhere. Danny wondered what had happened to her.

"Reckon we'd best go hunt for that yellow hen," he murmured to Red. "How about it?"

Coming to the creek, they swung up it. Danny studied the soft mud banks as he passed, and found fresh tracks of mink, coon, and otter. However, as nearly as he could tell, none had veered toward the clearing. Nor did Red, ranging through the beech woods, give any sign that he found anything amiss. A half-mile up the creek, he came in to join Danny.

It was unlikely that anything would carry food this far before stopping to eat, and there had been no yellow feathers scattered around. Danny swung into the forest, and waved an arm. At the signal, Red ranged out to hunt.

He came to a beautiful point in a patch of wintergreen, and edging up behind him, Danny flushed two grouse. He grinned expectantly. Ruffed grouse were the peer of all game, and Red was far and away the peer of partridge dogs. Shooting grouse over Red was Danny's favorite sport, and the fact that there were so many grouse foretold good things for the hunting season to come.

Danny swung back, paralleling the course he had taken up the creek. Red still ranged from side to side, finding and pointing another grouse. Then he found a covey of bob-tailed, half-grown young birds. Danny licked his lips. Unless it was freshly caught brook trout, there was no finer eating than young grouse. But the season was closed on them.

Aided by Red's keen nose and hunting instinct, Danny searched the beech woods thoroughly. He neglected no cranny or crevice where a raiding beast might have eaten the yellow hen, but he found no feathers and Red detected nothing except more grouse. The yellow hen, true to the instincts of game fowl, must have stolen her nest somewhere. He should know definitely in a day or two. If the hen did not come in to feed, and more chickens were missing, it would be proof that a raider was at work.

"Let's go in and see if Pappy's back from his bee hunt," Danny told Red.

Side by side they swung back toward the cabin and broke out of the beech woods. The five pups, disinclined to further exercise because their bellies were filled, sprawled in the sunshine. Sheilah wagged a dainty welcome from the porch, and Red joined her. Danny entered the cabin. Ross was at the sink, washing up. Two pails of wild honey were standing on the kitchen table.

"Hi, Pappy. Where'd you find it?"

"Trap Log Hollow," Ross said. "It was in a big old oak, and I had to chase a bear 'n' two cubs out before I could get at it. Right up in the tree they were, takin' turns dippin' their paws in. Never paid no mind to the bee stings, either."

"Mr. Haggin wants some," Danny said. "Will you take him a jar?"

"Sure. You saw Haggin?"

"Went down this morning. Had to find out where we stood."

"Well?"

"We've got a job. Mr. Haggin's going to put you

on the payroll, too. We're supposed to take one of the pups and make him into a hunter. That is, with Joe Williams' help."

"Where's Williams come in?"

"He's a dog trainer, Mr. Haggin said. We'll work with him and find out how he does things."

Ross hung up the towel and turned to Danny.

"Haggin don't figure we're goin' to train those pups the way Williams trains his dogs, does he?"

"I don't know. Why?"

"Because," Ross said, "the first time you take a whip to those pups is the last time they'll be good for anythin'. That ain't the way to make an Irish setter work for you."

"I know that."

"What'd you tell Haggin?"

"That we'd try it."

"Goshamighty, boy! We won't get anywhere doin' that! I'll grant you that Williams knows his dogs, but he don't know these red ones! He'll ruin 'em complete!"

Danny remained silent. Ross swivelled on his heels to look out of the window, and for a moment he did not speak.

All his life Ross had been a Wintapi hunter and trapper. It was a good life, the only one he would have wanted, but it was also a hard one. He wanted something else, something better, for Danny. Maybe taking care of a rich man's dogs was the answer. Danny could go far in such a job. When he spoke, Ross's tones were more gentle.

"I'll take some honey down to Mr. Haggin,

Danny, and have a talk with him myself. There could be somethin' in his offer. Don't fret."

Picking up one of the pails, Ross departed. Dully Danny stoked the stove and began to assemble the ingredients for a hunter's stew. He put them into a pot, poured water over them, added seasoning, and pushed the pot over a hot lid.

If Ross refused to accept Mr. Haggin's offer, then of course Danny couldn't either. They were partners. Danny watched his simmering stew. Then he heard Red bark and Ross came back up the trail.

"We talked it over," he said, "and there's somethin' in it at that. Push your mulligan on the back of the stove, Danny. We got things to do."

"What things?"

Ross turned his back so Danny couldn't see his face. "I told John Price that we'd fetch Sheilah and the pups down right away. Tomorrow we start workin' with Williams."

# 4. Joe Williams

The sun was high when Danny awakened. For a few minutes he lay drowsily, watching a fly that had somehow managed to get through the screens into the cabin, and that now hung upside down on the ceiling. It had been a cold night, Danny remembered, and once he had awakened to get another blanket. Now the cabin was warm. Danny sat up.

A rush of memory overwhelmed him, so that he suddenly knew what he had been vaguely trying to place when he awakened. Sheilah, who had been in the cabin for many months, was no longer there and the cabin in the beech woods seemed strangely empty and deserted. Danny's eyes strayed to the mat Sheilah had occupied, then he looked toward the stove. Ross was cooking flapjacks.

"Morning," Danny called.

"Huh," Ross grunted, "the way some people around here sleep, maybe they'd best practise to say 'afternoon' instead. Thought you were goin' to pound that pillow until next Tuesday, Danny."

"Wouldn't be a bad idea."

Danny swung out of bed and absently tickled Red's ears when the big dog padded over to him. He looked again at Ross. His father had had many dogs, but never one like Sheilah, and last night Danny and Ross had locked Sheilah and the pups in separate runs down at the big house. Still, though Ross felt the loss, he was not showing it.

"Haul your bones out of there," Ross ordered, "and pack a mess of these flapjacks into you. Half the day's gone and we start our new job this mornin'."

Danny laughed. "Don't be in such a sweat, Pappy. It's only twenty past seven."

"Well," Ross grumbled, "when I was your age we expected to have half a day's work behind us come that time. Don't know what you young whipper-snappers are comin' to. Rustle now."

Danny dressed in a hurry. The cabin glowed with warmth from the big cook stove, but little tendrils of cold air skulked about the windows and entered the cracks. Summer was at its height, but throughout the weather had been unseasonably cold. Danny washed and sat down behind the huge stack of pancakes Ross had ready for him.

"Cold night," he observed.

"Sure was, and it looks like we're in for a passable tough winter. Be a long one, too. Squirrels are already layin' up a store of winter grub. We'll see snow in plenty before the trilliums bloom again."

Danny tore into his breakfast, aware that now a certain eagerness had come over him. Gone were his doubts. Working closely with a professional dog trainer was really a wonderful opportunity. Dogs were to be his job, and he could learn a lot from Williams.

Ross finished and pushed his plate back. "I'll feed the chickens and pigs while you're feedin' your own face," he said.

Ross put on his faded blue jacket and his battered old black hat with fishing flies stuck in the band. He opened the door, and stopped short.

"Holy thumpin' wildcats!" he ejaculated.

"What's the matter?"

Danny slipped across the floor and looked over his father's shoulder. He whistled softly.

Last night he himself had locked Mike in one of the kennel runs down at the big house, but now Mike lay on the porch. He half rose, thumping the boards with his tail and beaming happily. Again Mike had performed the impossible, and escaped from a cage that should hold any dog.

"Seems to me I remember things," Ross chuckled. "They couldn't keep Red at the big house either, not when he'd rather be up here with you. That Mike pup, he's sort of stickin' by the Pickett family, too."

"Yeah," Danny said ruefully. Of Sheilah's five children, it had to be Mike the worthless who would come and seek them out. Then he forgot his displeasure. The fact that Mike had come back, and preferred the cabin in the woods to the luxuries of the big house, was enough in his favor. "What are we goin' to do with him?" Danny asked.

"Take him back, of course."

"You know what I wish?" Danny said. "I wish Sean, or Eileen, or either of the other two, was our pup to do with what we want."

Ross knelt on the floor and tickled the white star on Mike's chest. The puppy rolled over, playfully biting Ross's caressing hand. Danny watched, and because he knew dogs he understood something

about the red puppy. Mike had proven that he liked
the Picketts better than anyone else, but he wasn't
really anyone's dog. He was a rebel.

Ross straightened, and said, "If I had the pick of
the litter, I'd take this one."

"Why?"

"Because he's all dog. I'll grant you that he ain't
ever goin' to win any blue ribbons at any fancy
shows. But you and Mr. Haggin tried to get a dog
with all that's best of both Red and Sheilah in him.
Mike's got it. He ain't much for looks, but he's got it
inside."

"How do you figure that?"

"Look at him."

"I can't see it, Pappy."

"I've been wrong, but I ain't this time. If any man
ever gets sense enough to bring out what Mike's got,
he'll have a dog to beat the field."

Danny made no comment. When Ross fell over-
board he went all the way, and he had always liked
Mike. Maybe that was because few other people
did. Maybe it was because Sheilah was gone.

"Reckon I'll finish my breakfast," Danny said.

He did, and gave Mike a heaping plateful of food.
The red puppy gobbled everything and licked the
tin plate. Then he leaped up to spring at Red, and
Red beat a hasty retreat into the cabin. Mike pawed
enthusiastically at the closed door, then turned to
bite Ross's trouser cuffs when Ross came back from
the outbuildings.

"Well," said Danny's father, as they finished the

dishes, "if you're ready, we'll go let Haggin's trainer learn us about dogs."

"I'm ready."

Danny slipped a training collar over Mike's head, snapped a leash onto it, and fell in beside Ross. When Red would have gone with them, Danny ordered him back. The best trainer in the world couldn't possibly teach Red more about hunting than he already knew, and besides it was just as well to leave a guardian at the cabin.

"Damn!" Ross said as they neared the kennels.

"What's eating you?"

"I feel sort of funny. This marks the first time in twenty-five years that I've gone to do another man's biddin'. I sort of don't like the feelin'."

"You've been running the woods so long that you're wilder than a buck deer!" Danny scoffed. "You'll tame down."

"Hope you're right."

They swerved to the kennel runs, and came upon Sheilah, imprisoned in a run all by herself. Her tail wagged furiously, and she uttered anxious little whines. Sheilah adored only one man, and now she was telling him how happy she was to see him again. Ross thrust a hand through to stroke her, and Sheilah flattened an ecstatic head against the wire.

"All right, old girl," Ross said soothingly. "We all got to do things we don't like. Shucks, even dogs got to."

Danny unlatched the gate to Mike's run, picked the red puppy up, and thrust him inside. Unconcerned, Mike sat down in the center of the gravelled run, and started scratching his right ear with his right hind paw.

A second later Joe Williams appeared. "Good morning," he said affably.

"Good morning," Danny replied.

Ross nodded. The four pups, all in separate pens, waited expectantly. The trainer snapped his fingers at Mike, who turned his back on him with almost studied deliberation. Joe Williams frowned.

"I can't figure how a couple of champions threw a mutt like that. The other four are fine pups, but he's sure a mistake."

"It happens," Ross pointed out. "Why, I've seen lashin' big bears trailed by cubs that wouldn't be bite size when they were full-grown."

"Yes, but that pup's brain is stunted, too. I was out here this morning and the other four came right up to the fence. That one snubbed me cold."

"What time this morning?" Danny inquired.

"About quarter to six."

Danny said nothing. Obviously Mike had escaped after the place was astir, and had made good his escape without being seen. Maybe that was luck and maybe he hadn't wanted to be seen. Anyhow, it would do no good to say that the red puppy could get away whenever he felt like it, especially since Danny didn't know how he did it.

The trainer faced them. "I hope you two don't expect to learn any deep, dark secrets, or any black magic. As far as I know, there's no such thing. You have to understand your dog and work with him. That's all I know."

"Sounds sensible," Ross admitted. "That's about all anybody has to know. Can we see how you do it?"

"Come on I'm going to work one of the pups."

They followed Joe Williams along the line of kennel runs to a gawky pup who leaped enthusiastically against the wire. He continued to leap and frolic even after the trainer ordered him to sit. Joe Williams took a leash from its hook, entered the cage, and gently forced the puppy to a sitting position. He held him there while he snapped the leash onto his collar, but as soon as he was released the puppy jumped up.

"Sit!" the trainer ordered.

The puppy backed two steps and looked up, obviously not understanding. Again he was pressed into a sitting position and held there. This time he remained sitting while his trainer backed two steps. The leash dangled loosely. Then a wind-blown leaf scudded across the pen and the puppy started to race after it.

"Sit!" Joe Williams said firmly.

He tightened the leash, with the same motion tightening the collar around the puppy's neck. The youngster strained at the leash, still intent on playing with the leaf. Patiently the trainer pressed him to the ground, and this time the puppy stayed. Joe Williams backed away. After a second he said, "All right."

Simultaneously he snapped his fingers, and the puppy romped happily up to him. The trainer dug into his pocket for a bit of dog biscuit. He handed it to the puppy, who ate and licked his trainer's hand. Joe Williams turned to Ross and Danny.

"Patience and the right amount of firmness does it," he said. "They have to know who's boss, and at the same time like to work for him."

"Yeah," said Ross.

Danny said nothing. Maybe some dogs had to learn this way, but never once had he tightened a collar around Red's neck. He and his father stepped back as Joe Williams brought the puppy out of his run. Only one man could handle a dog. If two tried it, confusion was apt to result. No dog could serve two masters.

Naturally friendly, the puppy strained toward these two intriguing strangers and possible playmates. He came to the end of his leash and continued to strain. Using more than a necessary amount of strength, Joe Williams pulled him back. Without really hurting the puppy, the tightening collar closed about his neck and shut off his breath. The puppy turned, cringed slightly, and wagged an appeasing tail at his trainer. Joe Williams patted his head and ruffled his ears, and the next time the puppy tried to wander he went only far enough to let the collar tighten slightly. He kept one eye on his trainer.

"A field dog is worthless if he won't listen and obey," Joe Williams said. "Not that this one will ever be more than a passable gun dog anyhow."

Danny had already arrived at the same conclusion. The puppy was not nearly as good as the young dog that had come to the cabin with John Price and Mr. Haggin. Danny was relieved; plainly not all English setters were champions. As a breed they were like any other dog, with good, bad, and indifferent individuals.

Joe Williams tightened the leash, bringing the puppy to his side, and walked away from the kennels. They came to a field, and the trainer knelt beside his charge. He unsnapped the leash, but held the collar for a moment. Then he released the puppy and signalled with his arm.

"Go!" he said.

The puppy ambled uncertainly forth, stopping here and there to snuffle. Making a little circle, he wagged back to Joe Williams and looked up into his face. The trainer fed him another treat, petting him gently while he explained.

"Let me say again that patience and firmness are the key words. This puppy hasn't even a faint idea of what he's to do, but he'll get it if he snuffles around by himself. Probably any dog is born with more understanding of hunting than any man will ever acquire. It takes a man, however, to bring out whatever the dog's got."

"Some times," Ross observed, "I've seen the dog bring out what the man's got, too."

"That's right," the trainer agreed. "It happens."

The puppy, finding himself under no restraint and without any orders, ranged farther into the field. He picked up and threw a bit of grass, pouncing on it with all four feet and snatching it up again before it struck the ground. For a few seconds he continued to play the game he had invented. Losing interest, he wandered on, stopping to snuffle wherever there was an intriguing scent. Game birds, quail and pheasants, had been in this field and the puppy found the scents they left fascinating.

Then a rabbit burst from beneath his very nose, and the puppy forgot everything else. Eager eyes fastened on the fleeing game, yapping hysterically, he raced after it.

"Here!" Joe Williams shouted. "Come back here!"

The puppy, paying absolutely no attention, came to some tall grass at the end of the field and lost his quarry in it. Happily he cast around and around, trying to find the rabbit. The three men ran up, while the puppy continued his frantic quest. Panting hard, he ran to all the places where he thought it might be. Finally tiring, he wagged sheepishly to his trainer.

Joe Williams stooped and snapped the leash back onto his collar. He stood erect, letting the leash hang slack.

"Sit!" he commanded.

The puppy sat, turning his head sideways and still panting happily. A breeze ruffled the grass, and at once the puppy sprang erect. He strained toward the moving grass, thinking the rabbit might be there. Then he yelled in pain as Joe Williams, doubling the leash, slashed him across the back with it. The trainer struck again and again, until the puppy cringed at his feet. The pup hitched himself along on his belly. His tail wagged appeasingly. After a moment, when the lesson had had time to penetrate, the trainer stooped to pet his charge.

Forgiven, the pup showed his apology for wrong-doing, by leaping up and wagging his tail furiously. He reared with his fore paws on the trainer, wriggling every portion of his body and whining happily. Joe Williams gently pulled the puppy's ears, then as gently pushed him to the ground.

"You have to teach 'em," the trainer said, "and it's wonderful how an occasional licking will improve any dog's manners. I couldn't let him get away with this. If I did, he'd think it was all right to chase rabbits. The more you let him do it, the harder he'd be to break. A field dog that will chase rabbits isn't worth anybody's time."

Ross nodded. "Had to whale my hounds from time to time, too, mostly to keep 'em off deer."

"Any dog needs it," the trainer asserted. "Now watch, and remember that this pup's had a lot of basic training."

He unsnapped the leash and let the puppy go. Uncertain, casting frequent glances over his shoulder, the youngster edged forward. He turned to come back, then started out again. Intrigued by a sparrow on a fence post, the puppy stopped in his tracks, scarcely moving a muscle as he froze into rigidity. Talking soothingly to him, Joe Williams advanced to his side.

"All right!" he said.

The happy pup, knowing that he had something to merit praise, wagged a delighted tail and accepted another treat. He looked questioningly up, and when Joe Williams waved his hand, he raced into the field. A covey of quail, bursting like feathered bombs in front of him, shocked him into doing nothing.

Danny watched, and analyzed. The pup was intelligent enough, but that invisible bond, the confining presence of the trainer, was already being fashioned. Joe Williams had perfect control of his dogs and there was no doubt that he was a good trainer. He had not beaten the puppy severely. Still. . . .

Ever since Danny could remember, his father had had dogs and some were very good ones. But the dog that was more than good, the one able to understand what his master wished and who loved to do it, was Red. Red would not be the dog he was if he had been subjected to this sort of training. He had always been free to think for himself. Any dog that depended too much on a master never could have run Old Majesty to earth. Ross's hounds had failed partly because they recognized Ross as the source of all power and acted accordingly.

The puppy, free for the moment, gave himself over to playing and romping. He tore madly about the field, stopping now and again but never for very long. Finally, after half an hour, Joe Williams called him in and again attached the leash. The panting puppy remained close beside him.

"That's enough for today," the trainer said. "Given too much of any one thing except just wild running, dogs get bored and that spoils 'em. We'll call it quits for now."

"You mean," the puzzled Ross asked, "that we're all done?"

The trainer laughed. "Not quite. There's more to this than taking dogs afield. They have to be cared for in their kennels, too. I want you two to get the 'feel' of the whole business."

Inside the kennel building were large kennels; no dog ever had to be cramped for lack of room. At one end was a storeroom where food and clean cedar shavings for bedding were stored. This room was also a kitchen where special diets could be arranged. At the other end was a hospital stocked with medicine and a complete veterinarian's library.

All the dogs came noisily in from their runs when the men entered and reared to scrape their kennel doors with raking claws. Ross's eyes lighted.

He stooped over Sheilah's kennel to scratch her ears, then unlatched the door and let her out. Sheilah stepped out, staying as near Ross as she could get and sighing her pleasure. Things had gone wrong when she was brought here from the cabin in the beech woods, but now they were right again. She was near Ross.

The trainer frowned. "I wish you wouldn't do that."

"Why not?"

"It's all right to pet dogs, and to reward them for good behavior, but coddling is apt to make them misbehave. After all, it's working dogs we're after."

With surprising meekness Ross said, "All right."

He put Sheilah back and started cleaning cedar shavings out of the kennels. Danny chauffeured a wheelbarrow with which he carried the shavings to a dump far from the kennels. When he returned, Ross was busy scrubbing the kennels and putting fresh shavings in them. The trainer had gone.

Obviously Joe Williams did not consider it necessary for himself to get the 'feel' of kennel work. The only kennel he took care of was the one that housed Jack, the young setter whom Mike had fought. That was also the only kennel with a locked door, proof in itself of Jack's value.

At noon Danny and Ross had dinner with Curley Jordan and his wife, loafed a bit, and went back to work. No corner in any kennel was neglected, and by the time they were finished, everything was polished and shining. Joe Williams came in.

"All set?" he asked pleasantly.

"All set," Danny said.

"Good job, too. Well, see you tomorrow."

"We're all done now?" Ross asked.

"Until tomorrow, when we'll start on one of your red dogs. Right now I'm going to give Jack a workout."

Joe Williams stood expectantly. He was obviously waiting for Ross and Danny to leave before he brought his prize out of the kennel. The two Picketts took their leave, and Danny breathed happily when they were again in the beech woods. He was glad to get away.

This was not the way to feel, he told himself. Anybody who intended to make dogs his career had better learn all about them, and there was no better way to learn than by working with a professional who did know. But was a professional always right? If you wanted to break a dog of a bad habit, did you *have* to use the curled end of a leash? To set his own doubts at rest, Danny sounded out Ross.

"What'd you learn today, Pappy?"

"Well," Ross grinned, "anybody who starts to school, and don't tell teacher he's already had some schoolin', is pretty likely to start in kindergarten. Wish he'd showed us some of the things he's doin' to that Jack dog of his."

Danny smiled. Ross was merely saying, in his own way, that everything he'd seen today was elementary. But if Ross thought there were better ways to do things, he was not saying so. Maybe he had no such opinions and maybe he was merely keeping his own counsel. Ross never had been one to talk for the sake of talking.

Red, who had occupied the cabin all day, and grown lonesome doing it, trotted down the path to meet them. Danny watched him come, and his eyes lightened. There was certainly a difference between Red and the big English setters. Red had never known a whip, and not too many harsh words, but he had been told to watch the cabin and he had done just that all day. Would any of John Price's dogs, no matter how rigorously they were trained, do the same thing?

Danny doubted it.

# 5. Budgegummon

Coming awake in the half dawn of early morning, Danny folded his hands behind his head and stared at the slowly lightening windows. It was too early to get up, and the day to come had little appeal. All he and his father did now was go down to the big house and flunkey for Joe Williams.

They'd been doing it every day for two weeks, and so far they had learned almost nothing which Ross hadn't known when Joe Williams was in three-cornered pants. Trailing hounds or bird dogs, there were certain basic rules that applied to both of them. But some of those rules did not apply to Irish setters. Danny worried.

Mike, considered too useless to bother with, had been left alone in his kennel. But one by one the other four puppies had been brought out for basic training, and so far Joe Williams had been unable to teach them anything at all.

Where the English setters took their training more or less gracefully, Sheilah's children responded not at all. Danny thought he knew why. They had been born to work with a man, not for him, and they wouldn't do that until they were ready and until the man had earned their respect.

Joe Williams and John Price disputed that. Slow, they called the red puppies; they said that Irish setters were notoriously slow to learn. Given time, and hard training, all four would be reasonably good bird dogs, they thought, and that's all Mr. Haggin had asked. There was, they said, no possibility of a field champion among the four, though all of them would doubtless win honors on the bench. They had, according to the men at the big house, been born for dog shows anyhow.

Were they right? That question plagued Danny and had for two weeks. Sheilah was a better than average hunter. Red had out-hunted field champions, and the blood of both flowed in the puppies. This did not necessarily mean that they would equal their parents, but certainly at least one of the four should prove better than ordinary.

Danny fell into troubled sleep, and when he awakened again the windows were bright with morning sun. Danny rose, quietly so as not to awaken Ross, and padded across the floor on his bare feet. He opened the door to let Red out, stuffed kindling into the stove, sprinkled kerosene-soaked sawdust over it, and lighted a fire. Danny kneaded sausage—now that both Picketts were working and had little time to prowl the woods they relied more and more on store-bought food—and laid it in a skillet. He filled the big coffee pot with fresh water and put that over to boil. Mixing a batch of biscuits, he slid them into the oven. Then he pushed the skillet over a hot lid and went in to call Ross.

"Mornin' already?" Ross said drowsily.

"Come on! You're a working man now!"

"Sure, sure," Ross grumped. "I'm an expert at shovellin' cedar shavin's. Never thought I'd find myself playin' nurse to a mess of pampered mutts!"

"Hustle up!" Danny laughed. "Don't want to keep Joe waiting, do you?"

"Wonder what he's goin' to show us today." Ross was surly. "He forgot to tell me about a dog waggin' its tail when it feels good."

They ate, and Danny started to gather up the dishes. Ross wandered to the window and looked out, and when he spoke he again sounded like the cheerful parent Danny knew.

"Hey, boy. Come here."

Danny edged in beside him, and looked down to see Red lying on the porch. Then he followed Ross's gaze.

With a cluster of fluffy yellow chicks about her, wary as any partridge, the yellow game hen stole out of a cluster of brush near the feeding yard. She looked all around, then led her babies to where she had always found something to eat. Danny glanced at Red, who was intently studying the hen and her brood. If they were going to get her, it must be now. Danny spoke softly through the screened window.

"Fetch her, Red."

Red sprang from the porch and landed running. He raced straight to the hen which, true to game blood, made ready to die for her chicks. She flew in Red's face, beating him with her wings, but mother love was of no avail against the big dog. He closed his jaws about her, holding her tightly without injuring her, and started back to Danny.

"Mike! Mike! You, Mike!" Ross suddenly yelled.

The red puppy, again a fugitive from his kennel,

was racing full speed up the trail. He stopped so suddenly that his chin almost plowed into the grass when he saw the chicks. Leaping ridiculously high, he bounced at them and snatched one up. Danny opened the door and bounded from the porch.

Mike waited, tail wagging, eyes beaming. Danny knelt beside the puppy. If he hadn't swallowed the chick whole, Danny had to get it. If a dog acquired a taste for killing chickens, he was very hard to cure.

Danny pried on Mike's jaws. Mike opened them of his own free will and dropped the chick into Danny's hand. Danny stared incredulously at it. The chick was unhurt, scarcely ruffled. Holding the squawking yellow hen under his arm, Ross ran up.

"Did you get it away, Danny?"

"Look." Danny opened his cupped fingers.

"Goshamighty!"

"I can't believe it!" Danny said. "Let's try him again!"

Freed, Mike pounced upon and snatched up another chick. He delivered it willingly, and unhurt, to Danny. One by one Mike caught the rest of the yellow hen's nine children, injuring none and surrendering all. Danny and Ross stared in amazement.

Not one dog in ten thousand is born with a tender mouth, the ability to retrieve game without mangling it. Obviously Mike was one of the select few. Danny glanced down at the puppy, who was anxiously snuffling about for more chicks.

"Holy double gee! If he could only hunt like he can fetch, he'd beat the works!"

"How do you know he won't?"

Danny shook his head. "He just hasn't got what it takes."

"You seem almighty sure. Well, might as well go down and get those shovels hot, huh?"

"I reckon so."

Danny put the yellow hen in a slatted coop from which she could not escape and gave her chicks back to her. He fed and watered them. Then, ordering Red to watch the cabin, he snapped a leash on Mike's collar and they started down the Smokey Creek trail.

Nearing the kennels, Mike sat down in the trail and rolled his eyes. Danny twitched his fingers. The red puppy turned and, straining against the leash, tried to go back up the trail. Stooping, Danny cradled Mike in his arms and carried him. The puppy immediately started licking his face. Ross grinned.

"Maybe he thinks you didn't wash clean enough this mornin', Danny."

"Open his kennel!" Danny sputtered. "Let me get rid of him!"

Ross opened the door and Danny pushed Mike into his kennel. The red puppy retreated to a far corner, looked appealingly around, then lay down with his muzzle on his front paws. He rolled his eyes, obviously unhappy about the whole affair.

"Did he get away again?"

They turned to face Joe Williams, who had come silently upon them. Danny nodded.

"Yeah, He was at the cabin this morning."

"I'll have to do something about him," the trainer said. "Think I'll tie him."

He entered the kennel, careful to block the door with his own body so that Mike could not slip past him, and put a long chain on the red puppy's collar. He slipped the other end over a hook screwed into the wall. Highly disdainful of the entire process, Mike did not even get up. The trainer closed the kennel door and faced Danny and Ross.

"That'll hold him. Well, how about working another of your red wonders this morning?"

"Sure."

"Wait for me outside, will you? I want to bring her myself."

Danny and Ross went out. A few minutes later Joe Williams appeared with Eileen on a leash. Obviously he had been sweet-talking her, and when he stopped Eileen leaned confidently against him. The trainer stooped to tickle her ears and Eileen beamed gratefully. Danny approved. Nobody had to tell him that Joe Williams knew how to win a dog's confidence. Eileen walked to the end of her leash, but did not pull hard enough to tighten the collar around her neck. The trainer looked doubtfully at her.

"Sometimes these dogs show signs of intelligence," he admitted. "Come on. We'll get her away from the rest where she won't be distracted and see if we can teach her a thing or two."

They went to a quiet place behind the barns, and Joe Williams fed Eileen a treat. The puppy gobbled it, and thanked the trainer by kissing his hand.

Holding her front quarters up, Joe Williams pressed her rear firmly to the ground. At the same time, he commanded, "Sit!"

Eileen sat perfectly, and remained sitting until Joe Williams snapped his fingers. Then she thankfully gobbled her reward. The trainer looked puzzled.

"We'll try her again."

He issued the command, Eileen looked up, as though trying to understand, and wagged her tail. Again Joe Williams pressed her to a sitting position, and again the puppy remained until told that she could get up. The trainer's puzzled frown deepened.

"I don't know what's got into her. She never did anything before on command. Let's try once more."

Commanded to do so, Eileen sat. It was Danny's turn to be puzzled, but not at the puppy. Most Irish setters were very intelligent, and wanted nothing except to please. A professional trainer should be the first to see when a dog *wanted* to work with him. Eileen sat again, and again, upon command.

Then, without being bidden, she rose and walked to the end of the leash. Her attention had been attracted by a robin on a fence, and intently she studied it.

"Sit!" Joe Williams commanded.

Eileen acted as though she had not heard, and Danny understood that too. She had wanted to do what she had been asked, and she had done it. However, she could see no reason why she should keep on doing it when she had already performed satisfactorily. Right now the robin was the center of interest. The trainer tightened his lips.

"Bull-headed, eh? Here's where that young lady gets a much-needed lesson!"

Before Danny could protest, he struck her with the end of the leash. The puppy leaped like a startled deer, and turned when she came to the end of the leash. She struggled furiously, heedless of the choking collar. Her eyes became wild and rolling.

Without thinking, Danny snatched the leash from the trainer's hand, worked his way up to the trembling puppy, and knelt to cradle her in his arms. He turned angrily on Joe Williams.

"Don't you know better than that?"

Anger flooded the trainer's face. "I'll overlook this, Danny, this time. But let me remind you that these dogs are in my charge!"

"I'm not going to stand here and see you use a whip on these Irish setters!"

"Any dog needs a whip!"

"Not these," Ross put in heatedly. "If you ever try it again, while I'm here, I'll use it on you!"

"In that case," a new voice broke in, "perhaps you'd better not stay here."

They all swung to face John Price. Coming silently upon the scene, he had stayed to listen to the argument. Now his cold eyes were fastened on Danny. Danny glared back.

"That," he said slowly, "is the best idea I've heard since I started working here."

"Draw your pay at the house," said John Price.

Ross snarled, "Buy yourself another trainer with it."

He turned hotly away, and Danny ran to catch up with him. Side by side they walked back up the trail. For a while neither spoke, then Danny broke the silence.

"Pappy," he said tensely, "I couldn't do any different. I just couldn't. I can't stand by and see him ruin Sheilah's pups."

"Who's arguing with you?"

The tautness was broken by Danny's laugh.

"Hey Pappy. Why do I feel this way?"

"What way?"

"I sure ought to be down in the mouth," Danny said. "We lost the only job we had, but maybe we never should have taken it!"

"What d'you mean, boy?"

"Irish setters! We've got Red. We can put in the winter trapping and maybe buy ourselves a good mate for him. If we had pups of our own, nobody could tell us how to handle 'em!"

Ross looked quizzically at him. "Do you know what you're sayin'?"

"Sure I know."

Ross heaved a big sigh of relief. "I just wanted to make sure, because it listens almighty good to me. I never did like that job. We'll move to our Budgegummon cabin, Danny. That's right in the best fur country and we can string good lines. Course we ain't got much money now, but come spring we'll have 'most enough to buy a good bitch. Maybe we can even buy Sheilah!"

"That's the way, Pappy! We earned a living before we had this job, and we can do it again."

Ross said, "I'll go fetch Bide Clegg's horses and we'll start movin' right away! Ha! We'll spend out winter in the woods yet!"

Ross went striding happily past the cabin toward the upper end of the clearing. There were roads through the Wintapi, but Ross never used one when he could walk a trail. Few of the trails were man-made. Most were age-old traces beaten by deer, elk, and other game. Ross knew them all, and travelling them he could often reach a destination even before an automobile could get there over the winding roads.

Danny floated into the cabin. Sheilah and the pups were gone, but he and Ross were again oriented. They could start once more on the trail they had struck when both decided that, of all the dogs in the world, none could equal an Irish setter. Danny reached down to tickle Red's ears.

"You old flea cage," he murmured. "No more lonesome days for you! We're going to spend the winter in the hills—you and me and Pappy. How do you like that?"

Danny dug some boxes out of one of the sheds, lined them with straw, and packed the few personal belongings they would have to take with them. There weren't many. Budgegummon was an out-cabin, one of the places where Ross took hunters who really wanted to get away from the beaten track and where Danny and Ross stayed when they ran their far-flung trap lines. All the out-cabins were equipped with cooking utensils, bedding, and dry staples that wouldn't spoil or freeze.

They had to take a few extra dishes; Ross was sure to get some sportsmen in to hunt or for the late fishing. Also, they needed their firearms and tools. Then they must harvest their garden and take the produce along. Otherwise raiding varmints were sure to get it.

An hour later Ross returned with Bide Clegg's four brown horses. Since no wheeled vehicle could get into or even near Budgegummon, the wiry, sure-footed beasts carried pack saddles.

A grin seemed permanently etched on Ross's face as he packed the horses. Ross was one of the few Wintapi men who knew the packer's art, and Danny wondered where he had learned it. Perhaps in the Wintapi and perhaps elsewhere. Though he seldom talked about them, Ross had hit some long trails in his early days.

The packing completed, Ross tied the horses, one to the pack saddle of the other so they could walk single file on the narrow trail. Then he grasped the halter rope of the lead horse.

"High, low, jack, and go!" he said. "Come on, Danny."

They splashed across Smokey Creek, threaded their way among the huge beeches on the other side, and struck a dim path that slanted up the mountain. It was an old logging trail, built long ago by lumbermen. The little horses, accustomed to mountain climbing, plodded steadily along.

Though Ross took all the short cuts, it was still

four hours after they left the cabin until they came to the floor of Budgegummon Valley, splashed across the creek, and climbed the other side. A worn trail, beaten by generations of deer, wound toward the head of the valley. They followed that, and five minutes later were at the cabin.

It was built in a little clearing and against a hill. A few log outbuildings surrounded it. Poplars were scattered through the clearing and all about were the great gray beeches, the trees Danny loved best. They rested solidly on ponderous gray trunks, so huge that three men with linked arms could not have reached around them, and rose to a spreading canopy of branches. This was a fine and healthy place. Danny breathed deeply of the bracing air.

Red prowled off to investigate scents, and Ross and Danny entered the cabin. It was big, with a combined kitchen-dining room and a bedroom with six built-in bunks. Mouse-proof cupboards were still intact and an unmarked film of dust lay heavily over everything.

"Nobody been here for a long spell," Ross observed.

He checked the cabin's supply of flour, and the various dried vegetables and fruits that had been stored in sealed cans. None of it had been touched.

Catching up the two tin pails that were upended on a wooden bench, Danny walked to the creek and filled them. He washed the furniture, cupboards, and the top of the stove, with a damp cloth. Then he spilled water on the floor and scrubbed vigorously with an old broom. When he was finished it was clean enough for the present; they would finish when they came to live in it.

Late in the afternoon, with Red running beside him, Danny rode one of the horses and drove another back to the old cabin. He locked the chickens in their coop, and the next morning put them into two slatted crates. The yellow hen's half-feathered chicks he put into a box with their mother. Lashing one crate on each side of the free horse, he tied the box on top, and carried them up to Budgegummon. There the chickens were locked in one of the sheds, where they would stay until they became accustomed to their new home.

Hungrily Danny sat down to the meal Ross had ready for him. There were trout fried to a crisp golden-brown, potatoes garnished with wild watercress, wild honey, hot biscuits, and wild blackberries. Danny said little until he pushed his empty plate back.

"Well, we're almost moved, Pappy. Of course, there's still the garden and the two pigs."

"Yeah. Be a job drivin' 'em up here, too. Sure wish we could butcher 'em and bring 'em that way, but the weather's too warm yet and meat will spoil."

"I think I can drive 'em up," said Danny. "Red and I will go back this afternoon and make an early start tomorrow."

The next morning Danny approached the pig pen. Driving both its inhabitants all the way to Budgegummon would be no small feat, but Red was a fair herd dog. He had helped round up

Allen's half-wild cows and, Danny hoped, he would soon get the idea of herding pigs.

Danny ripped down a section of fence and went slowly into the pen. The two pigs looked suspiciously at him, grunting their questions, then walked unwillingly through the hole in the fence. Danny caught up a six-foot staff and steered them gently toward the beech woods.

He knew that this first lap of the journey would be the hardest and it was most important not to frighten the pigs or make them nervous. Maybe, when they got the idea, they wouldn't cause any trouble. Expertly Danny steered them into the woods, the bored Red walking beside him.

Suddenly, without any warning, a chorus of yaps swelled on the morning air and Mike swept in to help. Danny muttered under his breath, and turned frantically to head off the puppy. He was too late.

The frightened pigs each chose a different direction as they ran full speed into the woods. Danny emitted one hoarse, futile shout, then broke into a mad run as he sought to head one of the pigs. Hysterically joyful, Mike raced after the other one.

Red levelled out to run, favoring his injured side and catching his weight on the other, but running swiftly for all of that. He drew up beside the pig Danny had marked, reached out to take a firm grip on the pig's ear, and braced all four feet. The pig stopped, and Danny caught up.

"That fool pup!" he snorted.

Mike's clamor was dying in the forest, but he was

still hot after his fleeing quarry. Danny pondered.
The pig might stand and make a fight, and if he did
he could hurt Mike. But it was unlikely that he
would, and Danny had at least one captive. He'd
better secure it while he could. Red let go and the
pig whirled to race full-tilt back toward the clearing.
He lumbered across it into the pig pen, and lay
down in the farthest corner.

"Watch him, Red," Danny ordered.

Red took a watchful stand by the break in the pig
pen. Danny ran toward the place where he had last
heard Mike, and fifteen minutes later he met the
red puppy.

Having run his quarry as far as he wished, Mike
was coming back. Tongue lolling happily, as though
he had done a wonderful bit of work, he galloped
gayly up to Danny and leaped around him, evidently expecting congratulations.

"You!" Danny scolded. "You mutton-headed
idiot! A lot of help you are!"

He turned back, with the weary pup at his heels,
and led him down the Smokey Creek trail. Danny
turned Mike over to Curley Jordan.

"Lock him up, will you?" he asked. "He was supposed to be chained, but somebody forgot to do it."

Danny returned to the clearing, where Red still
guarded the prisoner. He picked up the staff and
again urged the pig through the fence. Red stayed
watchfully near, swerving to one side or the other
when the pig threatened a break. But the ear-
grabbing lesson had not been lost; the pig feared the
big dog. Danny urged him onto the Budgegummon

trail, and up it, but it was late afternoon before he reached the cabin. Ross met him.

"Where's the other one?"

"I wouldn't know. That fool Mike got on both of them just as I started, and I guess he ran one clean into the next state."

Ross grinned. "He does the dangdest things."

Danny leered. "You'd think it was funny if he ate your best boot, while your foot was in it. Well, he's lost us a pig. What are we going to do about it?"

"Oh, we'll catch it again," Ross said. "Let's put this'n into its pen."

The next days were busy ones. They harvested their garden, and used Bide's horses to haul all the produce up to Budgegummon's root cellar. But of the lost pig or Mike, there was no sign.

# 6. Fugitive

Mike stood in a corner of the run in which he was now imprisoned and pushed his nose against the wire. The run itself, ten feet long by four wide, led into the building where Mike had his own separate kennel, complete with new cedar shavings for a bed and a trough into which fresh, clean water ran constantly.

His movements were somewhat hampered by the long chain that was again attached to his collar and to a bolt near the kennel door. The chain worried him. He knew how to get out of the kennel run, but not when he was chained; he had been unable to solve the problem of slipping a collar over his head. Therefore it had been too long since he had been able to run as he wished. The last real fun he had had was when he had chased the pig into the beech woods. Mike remembered that, and had a great yearning to repeat it.

Mike went into his kennel to get a drink of cold water, and licked at the dish of food awaiting him. It was strange, crumbly stuff, not nearly as good as the meal, meat, and table scraps Danny had fed him, and he ate only enough to satisfy his hunger.

The red puppy had long since learned the layout of the kennels. He knew the exact number of runs, and the dog that occupied each. Across from them were the stock barns, and Mike not only knew that cattle and horses were kept in them but he had identified each separate animal by its own particular scent. Over all hung a strong smell of disinfectant, and Mike detested the odor thoroughly.

He was lonesome. Danny and Ross had not been around for many days, but above and beyond that he was thoroughly bored. The kennel run was not nearly large enough to provide an outlet for Mike's boundless vitality, and curiosity was driving him crazy. He had not yet had a real opportunity to explore this strange place where he was an unwilling prisoner, and he yearned mightily to look around the estate.

He came back into his run. Sean occupied the run on one side and on the other was a young English setter. Mike turned a calculating eye on that puppy.

He had tried to entice Sean into a romp, even though both would have to play on their side of the wire that separated them, and had failed to arouse even a spark of interest. Sean had done a lot of premature growing up during the short time he had been in Joe Williams' hands. He was not the same happy companion that had romped with Mike in the clearing. Mike hoped for better luck with the young English setter.

He pushed his nose harder against the wire separating the two runs, and whined in an unabashed effort to draw attention. Mike had all an Irish setter's dignity, but could turn it on and off at will.

The young English setter had his own ideas. Mischief twinkled in his somber eyes as he sat in the center of his run and gazed steadily toward the dog on his left. Mike barked pleadingly, and crouched with his forequarters on the ground and his rear end in the air. His tail wagged steadily. He barked again.

As though noticing him for the first time, the young English setter turned around. He squatted in the center of his run, pink tongue showing between his white teeth. Mike barked again, a rolling plea for attention. The young English setter rose and walked steadily to him.

They sniffed noses through the wire and two tails began to wag happily. The young English setter withdrew, crouched, and bounced about his pen. He looked over his shoulder to see how such a demonstration affected Mike, and saw the red puppy wild with joy. The young setter came back to the fence.

They reared, each on his own side. The young setter plastered his cheek against the fence, and Mike washed it thoroughly. Then he leaped down, snatched a stick, and began to run with it. Forgetting the last shreds of dignity and abandoning himself to play, the young setter chased him on his own side of the wire. Reaching the kennel, Mike whirled to fly back in the opposite direction.

Then he got a strange scent and stopped abruptly.

Three men were coming. Two were Curley Jordan, whom Mike liked, and Joe Williams, whom he did not. The third was John Price, who had not been near the kennels in a long while.

Mike watched them walk past, but he was accustomed to that because, except when he was fed, everybody walked past his cage. He sat down, head cocked to one side as he watched the men.

The three men stopped and turned around. Mike wagged his tail to show friendly intent, but made no move to go near. He trusted nobody completely; he wanted to discover these men's designs before becoming too friendly.

"This is the one;" Joe Williams said, "an out and out mutt. I haven't even tried to work him."

"What are you going to do with him?" John Price asked.

The trainer shrugged. "I've been waiting for you to tell me. If he was mine, I'd shoot him."

"Is he healthy?"

"Healthy as an ox, and just as dumb."

"It's wasteful to shoot a dog like that," John Price said. "There are always uses for one. Let's watch him run."

The three stepped inside the kennel run, and Mike wagged his tail a little harder while he stayed where he was. When Curley Jordan approached, Mike raised an appreciative nose to snuffle his hand. Curley unsnapped the chain, and Mike trotted to the end of his run. He stood watchfully, but bounded after a pebble when Joe Williams tossed one.

"See that?" the trainer said. "No size, no form."

"Well, crate him up tomorrow morning, Curley. I'll tell you where to send him."

The three stepped out of Mike's run and went to the next one. Joe Williams opened the door leading to the young English setter's run, spoke and the well-disciplined puppy stepped out. At another command, he came to heel. They went away.

Mike pointed a slim muzzle at the sky and moaned his heartbreak. Once more he turned hopefully to Sean. His brother, however, refused even to turn around. Mike coaxed with little whines, scraped enthusiastically at the dirt floor of his pen, and even retrieved the stick and rattled that against the wire. Sean paid no attention.

A jerky-tailed sparrow alighted on top of the kennel building, then flew down to the floor of Mike's run. Mike wagged a friendly tail. The sparrow was not the playmate he would have chosen but he would try anything to relieve the monotony of being penned up with nothing to do. He took an anticipatory step toward the sparrow, that flicked its tail and looked at him with bright, beady eyes. When Mike took another forward step, the sparrow flew.

Thoroughly disgusted, Mike threw himself prone. He laid his head on his front paws and rolled liquid eyes. Obviously this fenced run was no place to be. It was too small, too confining, and there wasn't any fun here.

Suddenly Mike raised his head. When the three men left, they had forgotten to chain him. He could get out.

But the time was not now. Whenever he got out of his cage at home Danny or Ross had usually caught him and put him back. He had even been brought back to this run several times. If he could escape again, he would do so when no one was around.

Mike bided his time, pinning all his faith on what he had observed to be the habits of human beings.

They were usually around by day but never at night, when they shut themselves in their houses. Obviously, if Mike escaped at night, he would be much better off.

The kennel man made his rounds and Mike gulped a few mouthfuls of the food put in his dish. He ate just enough to stay his rising hunger, for the food had no more taste than before. The kennel man left. Mike heard the kennel's main door slam shut and the metallic sound of the key turning in the lock.

The sun faded and the first shades of twilight made a pleasant summer haze around the buildings. Lights glowed in the big house and in the various tenant houses. Mike waited, watching the lights and testing the various air currents with his nose. There wasn't any hurry.

One by one, as the night chill made itself felt, the dogs left their yards for the warm kennels. Mike entered his, snuffling at the cedar shavings and taking a big drink of cold water. He lay down on the shavings, not at all an unpleasant bed, and slept for a while. A couple of hours later he padded back into the yard.

Most of the tenant houses, whose occupants started their day early in the morning, were already dark. Only a few lights glowed in the big house when Mike executed his escape plan.

It was simple. All Irish setters are possessed of a restless intelligence, but Mike's was tuned to a higher pitch than most. Since he'd been able to wriggle he had investigated every possible thing that came his way. It was this bump of curiosity, plus a willingness to try anything, that had taught Mike how to climb a fence.

He reared, stretching his front feet as far as they would go and feeling for two apertures in the fence. When he found them, he hooked his front paws over them and brought his rear feet up. Mike balanced his back paws on two more strands of fencing and felt for another hold with one exploring front paw. He brought the other one up beside it, then advanced his rear paws again.

When he could reach it, he grasped the top of the six-foot fence with his front feet and brought his rear ones up until his body was bent almost double. Then he kicked upward and outward, so he would clear the fence, and launched his agile self into space. Almost as supple as a cat, Mike twisted in mid-air and relaxed his legs. He struck lightly, easing the fall on limber muscles, and panted happily.

Now that he was again at liberty, he was overflowing with curiosity about this big estate. Even though he thought of Danny and Ross, and the cabin in the clearing, there was no need to go there right away. First there were things to be done.

A few clouds scudded across the clear sky, darkening the moon and stars. Mike padded happily on, knowing very well that it was going to rain but not caring. He had weathered storms before.

Mike went first to the horse barn. It was locked for the night, but he had no special wish to enter. He sifted the air currents drifting out of the barn, and after a few minutes had verified the number of horses in the barn and their arrangement in the stalls. He repeated his investigations at the cattle barns.

Dense blackness reigned now, and a drape of angry black clouds spread clear across the sky. Thunder rumbled and ragged lightning flashed. Mike paid no attention. It was a warm night and rain could not hurt him.

Suddenly Mike realized that he was hungry. Throughout the day he had merely nibbled at the food set before him, and had not eaten nearly the prodigious amounts to which he was accustomed. He sat down, trying in his own way to puzzle out where food might be found. Having never foraged for himself, he hadn't the faintest idea of how to go about it. His food had always been placed before him.

Restlessly Mike prowled back to the barns and investigated them thoroughly. He found nothing he could eat save a little calf meal that had been spilled out of a bag. Mike licked it up, and found the flavor not at all unpleasant. It was much better than the crumbly stuff offered to him in the kennel, but there was not nearly enough for a satisfying meal.

When a rabbit flashed out of the shadows ahead of him, Mike gave enthusiastic chase, but not with the idea of translating the rabbit into a meal. He chased it because he had always chased whatever fled from him, and he liked to see things run. When the rabbit lost itself somewhere in the tall grass outside the pastures, Mike abandoned the chase.

He made no effort to trail because he was not a trailing dog. The instinct to follow tracks left by any-thing except his master was only a dying ember within him, a function which he could not bring back to life because men who wanted his ancestors to hunt game birds only had made every possible effort to destroy other impulses.

Mike was very hungry now, but he still did not know which way to turn. He bit the tops off some young clover shoots and ate them. They had no pleasant taste nor did they seem to do anything to satisfy his hunger. Then Mike had a sudden happy inspiration.

Food had always come from human beings, and they would be in the houses. The only light that glowed was in two upper windows of the big house, but that made no difference. At full gallop Mike set off toward the house.

He ran up on the spacious front verandah and sniffed at the dark door. The scent of the people inside was very plain, but he could hear no one moving about or see any sign of people. Mike pawed tentatively at the unyielding screen door, but it was a massive thing, much stronger than the flimsy door on the cabin. It could not be wriggled or jarred. Mike pawed industriously, but succeeded only in leaving some long scratches. He sat down on the porch, looked plaintively at the screen door, and cocked his head from one side to the other. Then he scooted from the porch and ran around to the back door.

He was some distance away when a most enticing odor made him drool. Mike ran around the corner of the house, got the full impact of the odor, and licked his chops. A few light drops of rain spattered around him as he sat down on his haunches and looked up at three galvanized iron pails set on a concrete block about two feet off the ground.

They were garbage pails, and Mike's nose told him that the one nearest him held the remains of the big ham that had been served to the house's guests. But his nose did not tell him how to get it.

Mike reared, front feet on the cement block and nose extended as far as his stretched head and neck would permit as he snuffled more closely at the tantalizing odor. He got down for further study. The next time he moved, he mounted the block and reared with his front paws against the garbage can's rim. Eagerly he prodded the can with his nose, and when the lid moved a bit he pushed harder.

The can tilted, then tipped, and Mike leaped wildly backward as it fell against the next can. That, in turn, fell against the third. With a prodigious tinny clatter, all three cans rolled from the cement block. The lids clattered off.

Frightened, but not too frightened to rush in and snatch the greasy packet of ham leavings, Mike raced farther into the darkness as soon as he had it. He halted behind an apple tree and peered around it at the big house.

Upstairs, lights winked on. Two windows were

flung open and querulous voices called in the night. The kitchen light went on, the opening door framed a rectangle of light. Two men with electric torches came out, put the tumbled garbage cans back on their block, and went into the house. After fifteen minutes, all was quiet.

Mike tore his paper-wrapped plunder open and ate the large amount of fat and discarded scraps it contained. While rain splashed gently about him, he gnawed the last shreds from a big ham bone. It was a very good and filling meal, and after he had eaten it Mike felt sleepy. He found a warm dry bed, a comfortable niche beneath some irregularly piled lumber, and slept.

It was daylight when he awakened. The rain had stopped, but ominous clouds still scudded across the sky. Mike yawned, and looked out to see men beginning their work around stables and barns. Cautiously Mike emerged from beneath his lumber pile.

For a moment he stood beside it, wagging a placating tail and flattening his ears as he looked at the men. One saw him, and came slowly toward him. He was smiling, and seemed friendly enough, but Mike knew only two people with whom he would permit personal familiarity. The only time he had ever voluntarily let anyone except Danny and Ross handle him, he had ended up in a place he did not like at all. Mike had no intention of repeating that mistake, so when the approaching man would have grapped his collar, he ducked.

Mike glided away from the lumber pile toward

the horse barns, careful to maintain a safe distance between the men and himself. Presently he was confronted by Joe Williams.

The trainer made soothing noises with his mouth. Mike wagged his tail and flattened his ears, appreciating the show even while he remained wary of it. The trainer tried to coax him forward, but Mike would not go an inch nearer. The trainer's voice became noticeably less soothing and more angry. Mike backed away, and gave a great leap that carried him to one side when his would-be captor made a sudden dash. The trainer went away, Mike watching him warily.

He would be wise, he decided, if he left too. There were far too many people around here with sugar in their voices and evil in their hearts. Mike glided around a corner of the horse barn just as Joe Williams reappeared with a long-handled net in his hands. Mike levelled out in the easy, effortless run of the Irish setter, raced across the meadow, and slowed to a walk only when there was sufficient distance between the men at the barns and himself.

He paced easily across the meadow, stopping now and then to snuffle at mouse runs or places where rabbits had crouched in the tall grass. Presently he came to the edge of a beautiful green field and looked interestedly across it.

The field, carefully landscaped and seeded, was marked by flags and a varying contour of earth. Almost at the other end, a woman, a man, and two boys were busy at something. Much nearer, four men and four boys were equally intent. Having never seen a golf course, Mike could not understand what the people were doing. He was curious.

As he started across the green grass, his interest was attracted by a neat stone building at one side of the course. Mike sniffed hungrily at the entrancing odors that floated out of it. He had eaten a lot last night, but his puppy system needed more. Mike trotted toward the house.

He smelled glowing charcoal, and a man inside the building, but best of all was the odor of freshly ground beef. He came to an open door and looked in.

The man was in another room, and a rounded heap of fresh beef was on a table near the glowing charcoal. Mike walked in, reared against the table, and gulped great mouthfuls of the raw beef. It was delicious, the best meat he had ever eaten, but before he could finish it, a hurled coffee pot skidded across the table, followed by a stream of excited Latin phrases.

Mike beat a hasty retreat, knowing when he wasn't wanted and not caring to argue the point. Anyway, he had eaten almost all he wanted and perhaps the golfers would welcome him. Mike joined the four men and four boys, and took a spectator's seat far enough away so nobody could lay hands on him. He watched one of the men carefully place a ball on a tee, then swing with a club.

Struck squarely, the ball sailed like a bird down the fairway. Tongue lolling, intrigued by this wonderful new game which seemed designed es-

pecially for him, Mike sailed after it. He pounced
on the white ball before it stopped rolling, and
snatched it up in his teeth.

Tail happily erect, ears flying, Mike raced back
toward the men. He dropped the ball between his
fore paws and crouched, barking at the top of his
voice while he invited a game of tag. However, instead of entering into the spirit of the game, the man
who had driven the ball was yelling things at the
top of his voice. Suddenly he hurled a club straight
at the barking puppy.

Mike left, again not stopping to argue. All he'd
wanted was a game, and he had been most un-
civilly received. Obviously, nobody here really
wanted him around; all they'd offered him so far
was capture or bodily harm. Mike wandered disconsolately back to the barns, and went up to sniff
noses with Sheilah. After briefly greeting her son,
Sheilah stared wistfully at the trail leading to the
cabin in the beech woods. Two men tried to corner
Mike, but he slipped between them and escaped.

In the middle of the afternoon the rain started
again. A thoroughly soaked and weary pup, Mike
sought his nest beneath the lumber pile and tried to
sleep. For a while he succeeded, but with the coming of night hunger again drove him forth. The rain
had stopped.

Remembering the garbage cans, Mike went
straight to the kitchen door. The tantalizing odor of
meat, invitingly set out on the cement block instead
of tucked in a garbage can, tickled his nostrils.

Mike drooled in anticipation of the feast to come, then discovered that he was not the only one seeking it.

A big cat, a scarred veteran who ran wild in the woods most of the time, had also located the bonanza and was creeping toward it. Happy mischief lighted Mike's eyes, and he dashed at the cat. For a moment the big Tom stood his ground, then broke and dashed away toward the cement block with Mike in yapping pursuit. Mike halted abruptly.

He was just in time to avoid a cleverly laid net spread on the ground. The cat tripped it, and net and captive jumped sharply into the air. For a moment Mike looked at the enraged cat, then stared warily at the meat. It was still there, but this place concealed a great many surprises—all of them unpleasant. Mike remembered the one place where he had always received a loving welcome and the two men who had always given it.

It was high time he returned to Danny and Ross.

# 7. Lost Dog

The growth that overhung the trail to the clearing was still rain-soaked, and a miniature shower spattered down upon whatever touched them. A cold wind, forerunner of the autumn to come, had sprung up in the wake of the momentarily slackened rain.

Birds stirred little, contented to hug the shelter of leafy branches or evergreen thickets. Rabbits huddled deeply in their burrows, waiting for the weather to soften before they resumed hopping about their everlasting trails. Only the hungriest of hunters were afoot. Even the deer, that normally ventured abroad no matter what the weather might be, were staying in their thickets and wind-proof retreats. Almost the only sign of life was the red puppy going up the trail.

Mike was cold, wet, and hungry, but he had been all of those before and still managed to remain cheerful. Now his very spirits were crushed and his mood was in perfect tune with the black day. Since he'd left the clearing nothing had gone right, and he felt terribly in need of Danny's and Ross's sympathetic understanding.

Never had he felt so completely lost, but now he had definitely turned his back on the Haggin estate. It had nothing to offer that could be compared to the numberless attractions of the beech woods. If he could help it, Mike was never going back there again.

When he neared the clearing, he began to run. The dark clouds overhead rumbled and lightning flashed. The storm had merely taken a recess.

Mike reached the clearing, and a whimpering little sob of relief escaped him now that he trod again on familiar and friendly ground. He broke into his undulating run, leaped up the cabin's steps, and stopped short. Something was definitely and terribly wrong.

He remembered the cabin as a warm and friendly place. Now, even though it had not been vacated for long, it had acquired that empty look which all unlived-in buildings have. One window was broken and the open door swung as wind blasts buffeted it.

Mike sat down, lifting one nervous front paw and then the other as he looked dejectedly at the place he had come so far to find. He knew even before he entered that Danny and Ross were not in the cabin, and for that reason he was a little afraid to enter. Finally he bolstered his courage and went to the door.

Stopping half in and half out, he looked at the cabin's deserted interior. Of all the familiar things that had been there, only a few newspapers and bits of trash remained. They were strewn helter-skelter across the floor, and a couple of brown mice prowled busily about. When Mike went all the way into the cabin, the mice scurried toward their hidden holes.

Mike stood in the center of what had been the kitchen, his tail curled flat against his rump and ears drooping sadly. The things that had made the cabin familiar were not there, and most disheartening of all, Danny and Ross were gone. Only their scent still lingered.

Blown by the wind, the door slammed shut with a report that made Mike jump. He turned fearfully, shivering as he saw his only means of escape blocked off. His attention was attracted by something beneath the window, and he went over to sniff at a dead crow. Probably, in trying to escape the strike of a hawk or owl, the crow had flown against the window and been killed by the impact against the breaking glass.

Mike jumped nervously backward when the door blew open, then turned and fled through it at full speed. He felt a little better when he was again outside. The cabin was so cold, so cheerless, and so very empty. It seemed much bigger than it should and every breeze that sighed through was an echo of the happy sounds that had once filled the place. Nothing else, Mike had discovered, can be as empty as an empty house.

He was more than ever at a loss, and lacked even a faint idea of what to do or where to go. The scents of Ross and Danny remained inside the cabin, but outside the rain had washed everything away and there was no guide to tell him where his beloved masters had gone. He knew only that Ross and Danny had vanished without a trace.

There was no twilight, but only a thickening of the cloud-laden day and then it was night. Mike padded nervously to the end of the porch. Driving rain began to fall in great misty sheets.

Mike blinked into the rain and at the same time caught the scents borne by the wind. He smelled the pig, the one he had driven away. The pig had been running loose for only a short while, but already he was half wild. Now he stole back into the rain-lashed clearing to find food but he did not come openly. The pig had learned some of the ways of wild things, and knew that to be cautious is to stay alive and free.

Mike made no attempt to approach the pig, a creature whom he liked to chase but for whom he had no liking.

Despair and discouragement had momentarily made him forget his hunger, but now his appetite returned. Mike snuffled at the root cellar, whose door was also swinging open, then leaped from the porch into the rain. He ran to the root cellar and poked his nose within.

A mouse scurried past him and dived into a crevice. Mike looked disinterestedly at it, and resumed his olfactory inventory of the root cellar. It was heavy with mingled odors of the various foods that had been stored within it. Mike caught the distinctive smells of onions, potatoes, and cabbage. He drooled at the hooks where hams and sides of bacon had hung in the root cellar, and licked his chops. Finally he found what had attracted the mouse.

It was a two-pound slab of bacon, dropped and unnoticed when Danny packed the rest of the meat. The mouse had started on one end, and as the days passed he had eaten more than half. Mike picked it up, carried it near the door, and lay down to gnaw the fat bacon from the rind. He ate it all, then spent fifteen minutes chewing up and swallowing the tough rind.

Finished with his meal, Mike padded out of the root cellar into the storm, and was seized with a sudden, uncontrollable impulse to tell his woes to anything that would listen. He sat down, curled his tail around his rear paws, pointed his nose at the sky, formed his mouth into an O, and wailed as only a lost, forsaken baby can wail. The mournful notes were whisked away by the storm.

Mike stood up, tense and shivering, no longer a lost pup but a wolf protesting his woes. Then the spell faded and he was a dog again. He glanced sideways at the cabin, but stayed away from it. Then he turned toward the barn.

The barn door, too, was open and swinging in the wind. When the door swung wide Mike slipped in. The barn seemed friendly. Save for the fact that the tools and some of the fixtures had been taken away, it was not changed at all.

The same pile of wild hay upon which he had slept was there, beside two abandoned stalls that had not been occupied since the Picketts' mule and cow had been killed by Old Majesty. Mike turned wearily toward the hay, and again stopped in his tracks.

There was something besides himself in the barn, something alive and warm. Mike's tail stiffened and he lifted one foot, as though he were pointing birds. Inquisitive nostrils moved eagerly as he sought to identify the thing that was already in his bed.

It was a baby woodchuck, one of many that were annually reared about the clearing. Only this morning its mother had been caught by a prowling fox, and the panicky baby had left its home den. The barn had been an inviting refuge, and the baby 'chuck had not hesitated to enter. Now he was tense and frightened.

If the invader was hostile he would fight, but he had no wish to do so because he, too, was lost and cold. He felt as desperate as Mike for both company and comfort, so when the two babies met in the darkness of the barn there was no battle. The woodchuck rattled his teeth a few times and stopped. Mike wagged a happy tail, relieved that he was not alone, and lay down in the hay. The woodchuck, who would run as fast as possible from a dog as soon as he had more experience, snuggled close to him. The two lost youngsters had not yet learned that they were supposed to be enemies.

Mike slept happily, almost peacefully, more contented than he had been since he left the clearing. It was true that Danny and Ross were not here, and their absence left a great ache, but he was not without congenial company. A dozen times he awakened to snuffle his bed companion, then returned to sleep.

He awakened to find that morning had come and the storm had quieted. The baby woodchuck was standing in the open door, wrinkling his nose at odors that floated in, and presently he waddled forth to nibble green grass. Mike watched him go, but made no attempt to follow. They had met in the stormy night, comforted each other, and now each must go his own way. The woodchuck disappeared in some tall grass.

Mike had no realization that the baby 'chuck was going to find food in the grass. He was too busy trying to puzzle out the source of his own next meal.

He prowled back to the root cellar and inspected it thoroughly. The scents were still there, and the odors of smoked ham and bacon made his mouth water, but there wasn't any food. Not even a shred remained of the slab of bacon. Mike nosed along the floor, and turned up nothing at all.

A happy thought struck him and he raced out of the root cellar. The Picketts' garbage pit was beyond the upper end of the clearing, in a grove of white birches. Frequently Mike had recovered choice tidbits from it. He ran through the clearing into the woods, then jerked to a sudden halt, his attention attracted by one specific scent.

Forgetting completely the fact that he was hungry, Mike swung into the breeze. He worked carefully, head up and nostrils quivering as he traced the alluring scent to its source. The nearer he came to the big cock partridge he had located, the slower he worked.

He froze in a perfect point, nose stretched, tail stiff, and one front paw lifted. It was an instinctive move, one he could not help any more than a bird can help flying. Mike knew nothing about the more refined aspects of pointing and holding birds; the scent of partridge was simply far and away the most fascinating odor that had ever tickled his nostrils. With that odor heavy before him, he could think of nothing else.

Mike trembled with a throbbing delight that seemed to awaken every nerve and muscle. Only once before had he smelled anything so intriguing, and that time he had been too full of porcupine quills to savor the experience fully. Now he could, and he just had to get nearer to the bird he was pointing.

He advanced a step at a time while his body remained as tense as stretched string. Then he gave way to an almost delirious excitement and broke in a wild rush that was intended to overwhelm the sitting bird. He brought up foolishly as the partridge took thundering wing, and watched it as it sailed out of sight behind some trees.

Mike could not know that scenting a partridge at such a distance was a feat that would have reflected credit on Red himself. He knew only that hunting birds was a glorious pastime. Giving no second thought to the garbage pit and the food he might find there, Mike began determinedly to cast through the beech woods.

His search was swift but awkward and puppy-like. He knew nothing whatever of the habits of the birds he wished to find, and had no idea of the most likely places to find them. But what he lacked in experience he almost made up in enthusiasm. Mike raced wildly, nose always into the wind. A half hour after finding the first bird, he discovered another.

Again he snapped to a point. But again he let anxiety overcome him, and flushed the bird he had found. Mike watched it sail away, then resumed his hunt.

By evening he had found, pointed, and tried to catch, more than a dozen birds. Enthusiasm undiminished, but muscles and body wearier than ever before, he finally had to stop. When he did he realized for the first time that his hunger had increased ten-fold. Reluctantly he left the beech woods and headed off for the garbage pit.

The pig had been there and so had a small bear; their tracks and scent were much in evidence. Two such scavengers had left very little. Mike crossed and re-crossed the pit, hopeful nose to the ground, and found not so much as a crumb. Hungry birds and mice had gleaned whatever the pig and bear had overlooked or spurned.

Disconsolately Mike wandered back to the clearing and sought out the friendly barn. He had been hungry when he started and a day's hard hunting had made him ravenous, but there was neither food nor hope of food in or about the clearing. Mike walked restlessly back to the cabin, and peered in without entering. The cabin was more than ever a cold and cheerless place.

The puppy prowled all around the clearing on an aimless search, and when he found nothing he ate some grass. That didn't even dull the edge of his appetite, and tasted no better than it had before.

Suddenly Mike thought of the three garbage cans down at the big house. Remembering the netted cat, he was reluctant to go there. But perhaps if he went by night nothing would interfere. Mike started down the trail.

As soon as he broke out of the woods into the clearing he stopped to reconnoiter. He hadn't liked this place when he first visited it and he liked it even less now; only desperate hunger could have driven him back.

He started down through the meadow toward the big house, and was opposite the barns when a man carrying a lantern approached him. Mike stopped in the trail, warily watching. It was Curley Jordan. The lantern light fell on Mike, and Curley stopped.

"Don't look at me like that," he said softly. "I just do what I'm told around here. I never wanted to take Danny's dogs away."

Mike waited, friendly but unwilling to be recaptured. He kept a sharp eye on Curley Jordan, not understanding the words but knowing the tone of voice was amiable.

"I know why you ran away, and I don't blame you," the man went on. "I don't like some people around here any better than you do. Now wait a minute. I think you came back because you're hungry."

Mike backed farther into the shadows, uncertain now whether to risk foraging at the garbage cans. Perhaps he had better run back to the beech woods at once. Curley disappeared in his own house and almost immediately came out. Mike did not run because of the smell of the package Curley was carrying. He stretched his head toward it, and licked his chops when Curley put the meat and table scraps on the ground. Curley backed away.

"There you are, pup. I'm not going to try catching you. Eat it, then give my best to Danny and Ross when you find 'em."

Curley disappeared and Mike went swiftly forward to wolf the package of scraps. He sought out and licked up every last crumb, then wagged a grateful tail at Curley's house. Plainly he had one friend here.

Mike spent a lonely night in the Pickett barn, and all of the next day in an eager hunt for partridges. He didn't catch any or even come close, but his enthusiasm for such sport was still at a high pitch when night came. Again he went down to the big house and found the meal Curley Jordan had put out for him. There was plenty; Curley knew how much a hungry dog can eat.

Night after night Mike made his headquarters in the barn. The leaves began to turn color and the first frost left its white rime on the ground. Mike spent every day hunting partridges, and when he located one his procedure was always the same. He got as near as he dared, pointed, then rushed in to a hoped-for catch. Invariably the birds flushed before he got near enough to be even a faint threat. It was wild hunting that resulted in nothing, but Mike could stop doing it no more than he could stop breathing.

During his hunts, Mike did teach himself a great

deal about his quarry. He learned that they were almost always to be found in the forest, and that they ventured rarely into unwooded land. They liked the sun, and both mornings and afternoons were apt to be dusting themselves on sunny slopes. When night approached, they drifted back toward the thickets in which they roosted. They were omnivorous feeders, eating wild fruit, insects, acorns, beech nuts, and miscellaneous bits. Mike even learned to identify birds that he pointed again and again by their own distinctive body scents.

Mike also learned that the harder they were hunted, the warier they became. Some birds which at first he had found around the clearing had left it for the deep woods. With reckless enthusiasm Mike followed, going as deeply into the beech forest as the quarry he hunted.

One frost-seared morning he came upon a porcupine at the foot of a tree. Mike braked himself to an abrupt halt, remembering his earlier dismal experience with such a beast. He growled at the uncaring creature, then made a very wide circle around it. Safely beyond any possible threat, Mike ran to put more distance between the porcupine and himself.

A wild song of sheer joy suddenly burst from him. Completely by accident, he had stumbled upon a recent trail of Danny Pickett and Big Red.

Putting his nose to the ground, Mike flew full speed along that trail.

# 8. A Use for Mike

Danny Pickett left the cabin in Budgegummon with Red at his heels. He was going out partly to scout fur sets and partly to set a few traps for animals upon which he could collect a bounty. No good trapper, this early in the season, would even think of taking furs that would be worth twice as much after cold weather made them prime, but there was a two-dollar bounty on weasels, four on gray foxes, and twelve on wildcats. If Danny could earn thirty or forty dollars bounty trapping, it would come in very handy.

He crossed a small ridge, and stopped to nail part of a chicken head to a tree. While Red looked interestedly on, Danny set a number one trap beside the bait, staked it, and covered it lightly with leaves. He travelled on, setting traps at intervals. They were all weasel sets and no special care had to be taken with them. Weasels were voracious little beasts, and not afraid of human scent.

As he walked farther into the woods, Danny worried a bit about Ross. All his life Danny's father had waged a bitter hand-to-hand struggle with the elements around him, and had held his own. Ross, however, had faced too many blizzards, been caught in too many storms, had fought his way across too much deep snow. It was beginning to show. It seemed only a few weeks ago that he had been able to keep going all day and all night too, but now he was glad to seek his bunk right after supper. Furthermore, he seemed unduly depressed. He had loved Sheilah and her children and now they were lost to him. Although he said little, Danny knew that he brooded about it.

They hadn't done any hunting at all yet because the only seasons open were those on woodcock and waterfowl, and very few ducks and geese flew over the mountains. There were plenty of woodcock, but they were tiny things, not worth an expensive shotgun shell. Danny grinned ruefully. Hunting was properly a sport, but there were times when a man had to figure on getting the biggest possible supply of meat for each shell expended.

Red came padding back and looked anxiously at Danny. The big dog knew as well as his master that hunting season was at hand, and he was eager to be on with the real business of hunting.

"Few more days," Danny murmured. "Just a few more days and we can go after partridge, Red. Hang onto your tail until then."

Danny set a few more weasel traps and located good spots for fox sets near trails that ran through the woods. Then he swung down a hill toward a brook that ran into Budgegummon Creek. There were muskrat signs here, and many willow thickets where rabbits lived. The rabbits, and the trout in the streams, would attract mink and otter. Prospecting for fur signs, Danny cruised along the stream.

Red had been absent for some time, and Danny straightened to look for him. He whistled, and waited. Red never liked to leave a partridge he was pointing, but he would always respond to a whistle. Up on the ridge he had just left, Danny heard an answering bark.

He knitted puzzled brows, not recognizing the bark nor understanding what Red was trying to tell him. He knew all Red's various signals, from the happy one when he was teasing a porcupine to his thunderous roar of anger, but this was something new and strange. Danny whistled again, then between the trees he caught a flash of red fur and saw a dog racing toward him.

"Mike!"

A second later the near-hysterical puppy flung himself down at Danny's feet. He thrust his hind quarters into the air, laid his cheek flat on the ground, and pushed himself along with his rear legs. Then he reared and did an insane little dance. He rolled over and over, voicing his happiness at this glad reunion. Finally he sidled up to the kneeling Danny, slid his long head into the crook of Danny's arm, and closed blissful eyes.

Danny clasped his arm about Mike's neck while he tickled the red puppy's ear with his free hand. Mike sighed happily, and Danny swallowed the lump in his throat. The tale was easy to unravel. Mike always had been a genius at escaping any sort of confinement he did not like.

"You crazy pup!" Danny said. "You shouldn't have run away from your kennel!"

Mike danced again, wagging everything behind

his black nose and even twitching that as, in every way a dog can, he told Danny how glad he was to see him.

Red trotted down the slope toward them, and stopped to wave his tail gently when he saw Mike. The red puppy seemed in danger of wagging himself in two as he greeted his father. Red backed off and sat down, keeping a wary eye on Mike.

Danny looked at the puppy. Now that they had Mike again, what were they going to do with him?

Mike was thin, but looked hard as nails. He had never got that way in a kennel; plainly he had been doing a lot of running. He must have escaped a long while ago.

"Come on," Danny said. "Come on, you old muttonhead. We'll take you home for a while, anyhow."

Red again ranged out to hunt, but Mike stayed so close to Danny that his nose almost bumped Danny's heels as they struck straight through the forest toward Budgegummon. No smoke rose from the chimney; Ross had gone to Centerville for supplies and evidently hadn't returned yet.

Danny lighted fires in the cooking and heating stoves, mixed a batch of biscuits, and went out to catch a couple of trout. It was a long way to Centerville, and Ross would be hungry.

Ross came in just as the long evening shadows were beginning to fold into twilight. He pushed into the cabin, his face red from cold, and grinned at Danny.

"Sure smells good, boy." Then he saw Mike.

"Little cuss!" Ross was ecstatic. "Darn little cuss! Where in blazes did you get him?"

"I didn't. He got us. Came on Red and me in the woods. Guess he likes us better than John Price."

"Could be." A broad grin split Ross's leathery face. "Or maybe Price sent him to make up for the pay we didn't stop to get."

Danny grinned back. "Maybe that's it, Pappy. If it's not, he can come and tell us, huh?"

"Sure," Ross agreed, scratching Mike's ears. "That reminds me, Danny. Charley Spaulding's comin' here."

"To Budgegummon?"

"Yup. Got the letter today in Centerville. Aims to catch himself a big trout, he does. Says I better have one lined up for him. And if he gets it he'll pay. Charley always was that way."

Charley Spaulding was a wealthy sportsman who had hunted and fished with Ross for the past ten years, and now wanted to come to the Wintapi for the fall trout season. If he caught the trout he wanted, and it would have to be a big one to satisfy him, he probably would pay enough to solve the Picketts' immediate financial problems.

"How about some of the pools up on Tower Head?" Danny asked.

"I figured that's the place for him. Reckon you can guide him this year, Danny?"

"I reckon."

Danny said no more. Ordinarily Ross would not even have thought of letting anyone else guide

Charley Spaulding. Danny glanced sideways at his father; definitely Ross was not the man he had been. He was getting old.

That night the red puppy curled up to sleep on an old rug beside Ross's bed.

Two days later, accompanied by Red, Danny hiked into Centerville to meet the train that was bringing their guest. He bought a few extra provisions, then dropped his half-filled pack on the station platform and waited. At last the little mountain train steamed painfully around the bend, whistled its triumph, and Danny went forward.

A lean, well-built man dressed in trail togs dropped off the train. He carried a pack with three rods strapped to it, and a box of tackle.

"Hi, Mr. Spaulding!" Danny called.

"Danny! Boy, you've grown. And there's that— say, what happened to Red?"

"Fracas with a big bear. Old Majesty."

Charley Spaulding whistled. "You mean Red actually ran that old outlaw into the ground?"

"He sure did." Danny was proud, knowing that Charley Spaulding knew Old Majesty's reputation. "Red ran him plumb to a standstill. Here, let me split that pack with you."

Danny rearranged the two packs, being careful to put all the heaviest gear into his own. Then he hoisted it to his shoulders.

"All set?"

"Let's go. Hey, bucko, what'd you leave in this pack?"

"Half," Danny assured him.

Mindful of the fact that his guest was a city man unaccustomed to mountain climbing, Danny stopped to rest halfway up the mountain behind Centerville, then climbed on. They reached the great beeches on top of the mountain, and Danny struck down one of the dim little trails that led toward the cabin.

"Where are we going from Budgegummon, Danny?" Charley Spaulding asked.

"Your letter said you wanted a big trout."

"That I do. Know where there are any?"

"Biggest I know of are in the pools on Tower Head. They'll go up to nine pounds."

"Wow!" Charley Spaulding exclaimed. "Lead me to 'em!"

They pushed on, arriving at Budgegummon just as night was falling. Mike bayed an enthusiastic welcome. He bounded forth to meet them, but stayed warily away when he detected a stranger. Mike had had too many unpleasant experiences with strangers; he fell in at a safe distance behind them as Ross came to the door.

"You old woods-runner!" Charley Spaulding shouted. "How have you been?"

"Tolerable," Ross said. "That boy of mine didn't get you lost?"

"Not even near it, Ross. Say, this is a good layout you've got here."

"We like it. Come in and eat."

Red and Mike came in behind them, the puppy giving this stranger a wide berth as he sought his accustomed rug near Ross's bed. He stretched out, keeping wary eyes on everything.

Ross served one of his incomparable hunters' stews, that were never made twice of the same ingredients but were always delicious. Then Danny did the dishes while Ross and their guest relaxed, yarning about old times. After a while, Mike got up, paced across the floor, and snuffled at Charley Spaulding. The fisherman gave him a cookie from the table and Mike crunched noisily. Then he sighed and stretched out at the visitor's feet.

"Looks like you got a friend," Ross said.

"A rather strange one. Is he a thoroughbred?"

"Red's son."

"No!"

"I'll admit he don't look like much. He's still got what it takes. All I have to do is teach him some sense."

"How much of a job will that be?"

Ross shrugged. "Mike will come through, and when he does we're goin' to have the kind of pa't-ridge dog you read about."

"Wouldn't it," Danny asked, "be a good idea to go to bed? If we're going to Tower Head, we'll need an early start."

Danny and Ross were up two hours before daybreak, preparing a heavy breakfast. It was seven miles to Tower Head, with some stiff climbs facing them before they got there. Danny awoke their guest, and fed him huge quantities of ham and flapjacks. Then he caught up the pack.

"Seven miles there and seven back, that's fourteen miles to make today besides the fishing. If you're uneasy about it, we can take blankets and lay out tonight."

"I'll make it, Danny. If there's trout there I'll make it and back. I'm getting sort of old to be without a comfortable bunk at night."

"Good luck," said Ross wistfully.

Danny shouldered the pack, Charley Spaulding took up his fishing rods, and Ross kept Red and Mike inside the cabin with him. Long trips were hard for Red, and if Mike was allowed to go along he could be depended on to mess everything up some way.

As they went out, Danny took a flashlight from his pocket and lighted their way into the dark beeches. They walked for forty-five minutes in darkness, then the night began to lift and faint daylight enveloped them. As soon as they could see the trail clearly, Danny put his light away. He turned to look at his guest, who was walking easily with no apparent sign of weariness.

"We're getting there," Danny said cheerfully. "And there will be trout."

"That's all I—what's that?"

There was a flurry in the trail behind them, a rattling of pebbles, and Mike leaped enthusiastically upon Danny.

"Gosh-darn mutt! What are *you* doing here?"

Charley Spaulding grinned. "What are you going to do with him now, Danny?"

"Let him stay, I reckon. We'd lose too much time taking him back."

Mike, having made sure of his welcome, frisked around them a couple of minutes. Then he galloped headlong into the beech woods and was lost to sight. An hour later, he came up with them, tongue lolling, eyes happy. He had been doing what he loved best to do, trying to catch partridges, and he wanted nothing more.

They started the stiff climb up Tower Head, stopping as often as necessary to let Charley Spaulding rest. On one halt Danny's eye was attracted by a flash of brown among the beeches. A terrified squirrel sprang up the tree, raced to the top, and flung himself desperately into the next tree. Behind him, fully as agile and as tree-wise as the squirrel, came a lithe brown creature whose silky coat glistened in the sun. Danny's interest heightened.

It was a marten, a very valuable fur-bearer. Until now Danny had thought that there were none in the Wintapi. Where one was found there were sure to be more, and Danny marked the spot for future investigation. Farther up Tower Head Danny saw another marten. Then they came to the pools.

A spring rose on the very top of Tower Head, and pursued its course for almost half a mile among boulders and steep slopes. Then it levelled out to form a succession of deep, crystal-clear pools where huge trout lived. Nearing the downward slope, the stream went underground and reappeared at the foot of the mountain. Not many people even knew of the mountain-top pools, and fewer visited them.

The sun was high, lighting the first pool clear to the bottom, when Danny led his guest cautiously to it. They peered over the edge, and Charley Spaulding sucked in his breath.

There were more than a dozen trout in the pool, and the smallest would have made a fine catch anywhere. The biggest were monsters, an angler's dream come true. Danny backed slowly away from the pool.

"They're all yours now," he said. "Go to it."

"Just give me fishing room!"

While Danny built a small fire, Charley Spaulding rigged a rod and leafed carefully through his tackle box. He tied a fly to the leader and cast. There was a hopeful swirl in the pool, but nothing else. Spaulding cast again, then six times more, then changed his fly.

Danny watched him hopefully. He was a superb fisherman, and had almost every known fly, but none of them seemed to tempt the big trout in the Tower Head pool. As cast after cast failed, Danny's heart sank. He had wanted his guest to catch one of the big trout. Spaulding had promised a handsome bonus if he did, and the Picketts needed money. But at noon, still without even a fair rise, Spaulding came to eat the hot meal Danny had prepared.

After eating, he went right back to fishing. Patiently he changed and re-changed lures: bucktails, spinners, streamers, dry and wet flies. Danny's hopes sank lower. If there was any known lure for trout it was in the tackle box and had been tried without success. Danny glanced at the lowering sun; it was nearly time to start back if they would reach Budgegummon before dark.

Mike, tired out from his latest hunt, came in and sat contentedly near Danny. Keeping anxious eyes on the fisherman, Danny fondled Mike absently. Then he took a snelled hook from his pocket, unravelled a thread from his trousers, and began to work with his knife.

The fisherman was still beside the pool, still casting. Then he reeled in his line and came back.

"Nothing doing," he announced. "They're there, but they just aren't biting."

"Have you tried everything?"

"Twice."

"Trout do the darnedest things," said Danny. "Now if you could cast with a bucktail, set it just right at the head of the pool, and work it right, you still might tie into one of those big lunkers."

"Danny, I've got two dozen bucktails and I've set every one of them just right."

"Mind giving this one a whirl?"

Charley Spaulding looked at the fly Danny handed him, and smiled tolerantly. Danny gulped. "I know it doesn't look like much, but try it."

"All right."

He attached the bucktail to his leader and walked back to the pool. He cast, retrieved, and cast again. On the second cast, the pool seemed to explode.

Charley Spaulding set his hook, and expertly played the big trout. He handled it like the master he was, giving line when necessary but taking every advantage. Slowly he brought the fish in, and scooped it up in his net. His eyes shone as he looked at his prize, then he turned to Danny.

"Just what was that lure?"

"Oh, something I thought might work."

He really had thought that conditions were right for such a bucktail. But when everything else failed, a big trout had been taken on a lure fashioned from a hook, a bit of unravelled thread, and red hairs from a dog's tail.

# 9. Hero Worshipper

Charley Spaulding left Budgegummon with the biggest trout he had ever taken. He had paid Danny fifty dollars and given him one of his own rods. It was a bonus, he said, for the best fishing trip he remembered and the best bucktail he had ever seen. That much money was more than enough to take care of the Picketts' immediate needs.

After breakfast the next morning, rifle under his arm and sheathed knife at his belt, Ross went away to get the pig that was still running loose in the forest. When Mike would have followed, Danny grabbed him by the scruff of his neck and held him back while he closed the door. The wriggling puppy whined, knowing that Ross was going away and anxious to be with him. Red looked on, disgusted with the antics of his son.

"Cool off," Danny advised. "Take it easy, Mike. You're going to stay right here with me."

Danny finished his breakfast, tidied up the cabin, and washed the dishes. Then he slipped a choke collar over Mike's head, snapped a leash onto it, and took one of Ross's razor-sharp axes from the rack.

Red sidled softly out and away as soon as the door was opened, but Mike leaped against the restraining leash. Front paws cutting the air, he reared and snuffled in the direction Ross had taken. Danny held firmly to the leash. If the red puppy was ever going to be even a passable hunter he had to have some formal training and it might as well start right now.

Mike continued to strain, unwavering in his determination to be away. The tightening collar shut off his breath, but it was not that which finally distracted his attention. It was a partridge that sailed across the clearing.

Closely pursued by a hunting hawk, the partridge hugged the earth. He barely skimmed bushes and stones as he dodged and twisted to elude the hawk's strike. The hawk made a false descent and Danny watched the wily partridge sail into a grove of aspens and disappear. Then he looked at Mike, puzzled.

The puppy had gone wild, straining against the leash and making whimpering little noises. It was incredible to suppose that he had identified the partridge by sight; he had merely seen two flying birds. He must have caught the scent, Danny decided, and that in itself was a tribute to a fine nose.

Starting toward the poplars in which the partridge had disappeared, the puppy paid no attention to the hawk when it finally flew away. When Danny started toward the tree he wished to cut, a dead hickory that lay in the general direction of the poplars, Mike paced willingly beside him. Danny tied him to a small tree, and Mike continued to stare at the poplars. Danny scratched his head.

Mike might have smelled the partridge while it was flying across the valley, for it had passed quite near the cabin, but he could not possibly have scented it after the bird alighted among the poplars. Still, he seemed to know it was there.

Even Red did not possess a better eye for marking game down, and Red was far and away the best partridge dog ever to be in the Wintapi. That a puppy should equal him in any respect was little short of amazing. Danny swung his axe against the dead hickory while he continued to steal covert glances at Mike.

The puppy continued to face away, all eager interest centered on the poplar grove. Finally Danny laid his axe down and unfastened the leash. The liberated puppy raced toward the poplars, running at full speed and leaping all obstacles in his path. Danny watched him in amazement. Most hunting dogs cast back and forth until they find a scent, and not one in a thousand has enough hunting sense to mark game. But Mike could. Red was the only other dog Danny had ever seen that hunted in such a fashion; the red puppy had a lot of his father in him. Ross was at least partly right.

Mike stopped running to walk, then slowed to a near crawl. He edged forward, while Danny watched every move. The puppy was exercising so much inborn art and finesse that time seemed to stop. He snapped to a perfect point, and Danny gasped. It was almost as though Red hunted again. Then Mike broke and ran.

It was no nervous, unpremeditated break such as might be expected from the usual inexperienced puppy. Mike planned his break in a deliberate attempt to catch the bird he was stalking. The partridge flushed. Head up, tail stiff, Mike raced along beneath it. Puppy and partridge disappeared.

Danny shook his head. Flushing and chasing birds was a fault that might be remedied in any ordinary dog, but Mike had his own mind and will. Whipping and beating would only make him rebellious, and Danny had no inclination to train any dog in such a fashion anyway.

Turning the problem over in his mind, Danny picked up his axe and resumed chopping the dead hickory. Mike had Red's old speed and dash, and the Irish setter strength, but he lacked something that he must have before he could even be considered a hunter. He was a rebel, a wild, bull-headed rebel who had never bothered to consider anything except himself.

Mike came back just as Danny finished cutting the dead tree into sections Ross could use in his smoke house. The puppy was panting hard, but it was very obvious that he had had a delightful time. There was no hang-dog sheepishness about him, either. He wagged up to Danny and threw himself down on the cool grass beside Red, who had already come in from his own wanderings.

"Tired out, eh?" Danny asked. "Maybe you've got a right to be. Bet you've run fifteen miles since leaving me. I never did see a dog with so much get to him and so few brains."

Shouldering his axe, with Mike trailing beside him and Red following, Danny started back to the cabin. When they reached the clearing, Mike left his side and raced away at full speed until he disappeared in the forest. Probably he had smelled Ross coming.

Danny kindled a fire, washed up, and put water over to heat. Red came in to stretch out beside the stove, and a moment later raised his head. Danny went to the door.

Ross was leading one of Bide Clegg's horses, with the dressed pig on it. Mike was running around and around him; he still had plenty of spirit left. Danny went out to help his father.

They hung the dressed pig in a tree, and Danny felt again that respect which Ross's woodcraft always inspired. At best, butchering hogs was not easy or simple and Ross had had only primitive tools. Still the carcass was as clean as any professional butcher could have made it. Ross stepped back.

"There. Give it time to mellow and we'll have smoked ham and bacon. Did you chop my hickory wood?"

"Yup."

"Good. I'll haul it in the mornin', then take Bide's horse back. Reckon we won't need him any more."

"I won't anyway," Danny said. "I aim to get in a day's hunt, then hit into the big woods for a spell."

"Where you goin', boy?"

"Just cruising around," Danny evaded.

He hadn't told his father about the marten on Tower Head. There always had been a friendly rivalry between the two, and it would be a feather in Danny's cap if he could, unannounced, bring in a nice catch of marten. Also, if Ross knew of the

marten, he would insist on going along and Danny
did not want him to climb Tower Head. To avoid
any further questions, Danny changed the subject.

"Pappy, what do you really think of that Mike
pup?"

"He'll beat the field."

"He's got the heart, nose, and speed," Danny admitted. "I had that shown to me today. How about
the rest?"

"What rest?"

"A hunting dog's not worth the bristle off a pig's
back unless he'll pay some heed to the man with
him."

"I thought of that, too," Ross admitted. "He is
sort of bull-headed."

"*Sort* of bull-headed! I never saw a dog more set
on having his own way! We might take it out of him,
but how do we take out the bad things and leave
the good?"

"Ask Joe Williams," Ross grinned.

Danny grunted. "How about a training collar—
not just a choke—and a long rope?"

"Try it, boy."

The next morning Danny slipped a training collar
over Mike's head and attached a fifty-foot length of
clothesline to it. When Red tried to go out with
them, Danny ordered the big dog back. The red
puppy strained to the very end of the short length
of rope Danny let him have and began investigating
various fascinating scents. Danny stopped him
gently.

"Whoa!" he said.

Mike stopped and looked questioningly around at Danny. He started up again, pulling to one side to inspect some object lying there. Again Danny stopped him, repeating the command as he tightened the rope. Mike came reluctantly in to walk at Danny's side. A chipmunk flashed ahead of them and the red puppy leaped at it. Danny stopped him as gently as he could.

"Whoa, Mike."

The puppy shook his head, as though testing the collar and rope. When he started out again he did so easily, keeping the collar loose by not exerting any pressure against it. Danny felt encouraged. Mike seldom displayed much intelligence, but today he was not being fool enough to choke himself unnecessarily. Why?

With almost any other dog Danny would have known exactly what to do, but Mike was more than ever an enigma. Yesterday he had fought the leash hard, today he refused to strain against the harsher training collar. Danny let out a little more slack and the puppy trotted away.

"Whoa," Danny said softly.

Mike stopped in his tracks, turning as though inquiring what he wanted. After only three lessons, he responded as perfectly as any puppy could to the command to stop. Danny twitched his fingers and the red puppy walked in to have his ears scratched. He was a model of canine deportment, but Danny wasn't fooled. Neither people nor dogs changed suddenly overnight.

"Wish I knew what you're thinking," Danny murmured. "Sure wish I did. Reckon I'll take you into partridge cover and find out how you act there."

Mike walked amiably beside him, not even tugging at the rope, as Danny quartered up a beech ridge. This was one of the years' great harvests. The beech trees had borne a lavish crop, and tons of ripe brown nuts lay among the litter on the forest floor. Everything from furtive mice to lumbering bears were making free use of the great plenty cast down among them. There were squirrels by the dozen, and once Danny caught sight of an antlered buck sneaking away.

Mike sniffed at all the tracks, reading with his nose the stories of the animals that had left them. But it was not the passionate interest of an eager hunter. Suddenly he stopped short.

He stood, head up, still as a carven statue, while he read some fascinating tale brought to him by a stray breeze. A second later he swung at right angles to the course they had been following. He went swiftly but softly, making no more noise than he could help. He seemed to have forgotten Danny, and everything else, except the game he was working.

Danny let him go, paying out more rope as Mike got farther away and doing nothing to interfere with the puppy's hunt. Mike came to the end of the rope, and pulled hard.

"Whoa, Mike."

The red puppy pulled harder, scraping with all four feet as he sought freedom. Danny ran to keep up, and Mike kept the rope taut. He snapped to a point so perfect that Danny again could not help thinking of Red. Then he broke.

Danny held the rope with both hands, talking to and trying to soothe the frantic puppy on the other end. Two partridges took wind and Mike redoubled his efforts. He rolled over and over, tangling himself in the rope, and paying no attention to Danny's voice. Partridges were in the offing.

Mike strained harder, tightening the collar until his breath came in labored, audible grunts. His tongue lolled out, almost brushing the ground. His eyes were distended, but still he tried to pull even harder.

Eyes intent on the puppy, Danny worked himself up the rope. He did not even see the protruding tree root until it was too late, and when he stumbled he flung out both hands to catch himself.

The rope slipped from his grasp, and Mike raced out of sight.

When Mike ran away from Danny, he did so because he could do nothing else. The intoxicating smell of partridges was hot in his nostrils, and he would fight ropes, training collars, or anything else, to respond to that scent.

The trailing rope whipped about bushes and trees in his path, and slowed him to some extent, but Mike never even thought of the rope or of the sudden jerk on his neck every time it tightened. He had marked the brace of partridges down and wished to get near them once more. Nothing else mattered.

Mike wheeled suddenly and cut at an angle to the direction he had been taking. He had already taught himself that partridges did not always alight where they seemed to, and a breeze blowing in from the side brought him scent of the pair he had just flushed.

They had alighted among a cluster of huge beech trees. As Mike neared them, and the scent strengthened, he slowed his wild flight. This, the delicious moment when he neared the game he sought, was the climax of every hunt. The moment before the final pounce was a thrilling one, filled with something that satisfied the puppy's deepest longings.

As he came closer, he marked the birds' exact location. They sat in the leaves, heads up, fan tails spread, tense wings ready for instant flight. So perfectly did they blend with their surroundings that it was almost impossible to see them, but Mike did not rely on his eyes. His nose told him where the game was and he used that knowledge to his own advantage.

The partridges were between two beech trees, with a boulder on the far side and a small bush on the near. Mike approached from the boulder, knowing he would find no leaves on it and therefore he would make less noise. He stopped, edged forward, then snapped into a point.

He himself could not have known why he did. Perhaps it was a survival of some past age when Mike's ancestors stalked birds successfully, and the freezing point was part of that stalk. Perhaps his brain was magnetized by nearness to the game he sought. It might even have been something bred into him by men who wanted bird-hunting dogs.

Mike did not hold his point for long. There was something urging him on, something over which he had no control. He had found his game and now he must catch it. Mike put all the supple strength of his young body into a forward leap. He had chased hundreds of birds without ever catching one, but he never gave up trying.

These birds, however, knew how to evade a pursuer. Again they angled sharply from the course they had been taking and Mike lost them. For a little while he cast enthusiastically back and forth, hoping to find them again. When he could not, his enthusiasm remained undampened. There were thousands of partridges in the beech woods and he could always try to catch another.

Mike careened happily through the beeches, looking for more birds to stalk. Suddenly his head came erect and his nose twitched happily; partridges were dusting themselves about fifty yards ahead. He started softly toward them, leaped over a fallen aspen, and halted abruptly.

The trailing end of the rope had whipped around a tough laurel stalk and entangled itself. Mike sat down, pondering this unwelcome development. He lunged forward, and not only tightened the collar around his neck but alarmed the partridges. They left their dust bath and ran through the laurel.

At the sight, the driving urge, the fierce will to hunt, triumphed over everything else and Mike strained with all his strength. He reared, shutting off his own breath as he did so but not caring. He scraped the hard earth and rolled over and over. The rope tightened itself about the laurel bush.

Suddenly Mike stopped struggling to bristle. The changing wind brought him the odor of a prowling coyote. He was not afraid of coyotes, but he was angry because this one was stalking the same partridges he wanted.

He sat down, head alert, while he followed the rival hunt. The coyote was silent as a cloud, and only the fact that he had the scent enabled the red puppy to follow him at all. As he neared the partridges he went more slowly and carefully; the coyote knew his game and his skill and patience were endless. This sort of hunting had been born in him, and he was far more cunning at it than any domesticated dog could ever be.

Mike knew when the coyote stopped just short of the partridges. This was the freeze, the same as Mike's point, except that the coyote was crouching so low to the earth, and blended so well with his surroundings, that only the sharpest of eyes could have seen him. This was the tense moment preceding the kill, and the coyote wanted to be certain of where and how to pounce before he leaped in.

He sprang forward and upward, and intercepted one of the birds in flight. It was not accident; the coyote knew there were three birds ahead of him and he had decided in advance how they would fly. Bearing his prey down, he killed it and trotted away with the bird dangling from his jaws.

Mike sat mystified but fascinated. A great admiration seized him; plainly coyotes could do what he longed to do but could not.

Now that both coyote and partridges were gone, he could give some attention to his own predicament. Mike pulled tentatively against the rope, and again succeeded only in choking himself. He eased the strain by backing up, and looked back at the slackened rope, beginning to worry a little. He had been tied before, but never in a forsaken place such as this one. Anxiously he snuffled the air currents, hoping to get Danny's scent. Danny might come, and the very hope restored some of the red puppy's waning confidence. He stretched out in the laurel, dozing fitfully and raising his head frequently. Nothing came; he was deserted in the woods.

Mike got up to beat a restless circle within the limits of his tether. Plainly ropes were a curse. He must be very careful about allowing anybody ever to put another one on him.

Night came, and with it Mike's loneliness increased tenfold. Carefully he investigated the rope, looking it over from the place where it dangled from his collar to the place where it was snarled in the laurel. But not until another half hour elapsed did he have a happy inspiration.

Many times before he had chewed ropes in two, but until now it hadn't occurred to him to chew this one because no human had tied him. The rope had entangled itself, something new in Mike's experience. Besides, until now he had hoped that Danny would come. Since he had not, something had better be done soon. Selecting a place about three feet from his collar, Mike started chewing the rope. At last it parted, and the next time he tried to walk away he could do so.

Mike broke into a swift trot, but instead of heading straight for the cabin he started back toward the place where he had left Danny. He found Danny's tracks and followed them to the cabin. The windows were alight and wood smoke sweetened the air. Mike scratched on the door.

"He's here, Pappy," Danny said, opening the door. "You crazy red pup. I see you got caught and chewed yourself loose. Didn't know you had that much sense."

Mike wagged happily into the cabin. After an afternoon of anxiety it was wonderful to be back with the two people he loved. He went over to receive Ross's caress, sniffed noses with Red, and stretched full-length on his rug.

Early the next morning Mike followed Red out of the cabin. The puppy made a few experimental nips at Red's ears and tail, then raced around him a couple of times. As usual, he failed to entice the older dog into a game and went off on more interesting business. He snuffled at the tree where the pig hung, and contemptuously scratched dirt with his feet. Then he looked sidewise at Red to see how such a demonstration affected him.

Instead of admiring his son, Red was snuffling at

a bunch of frost-withered weeds. Had there been anything more interesting to do, Mike would have done it. But there was nothing else, so he trailed indifferently after his father. Mike looked around to see if Danny or Ross would come out of the cabin and take him for a walk, and when neither appeared he continued to follow Red.

There was no filial affection in the act, for never once had it occurred to Mike that he had a father. He liked Red and willingly accorded him his place as an important part of the family, but he also regarded him as a rather dull and stodgy creature that never knew the joys of bouncing up and down or running for the sheer pleasure of running. Red was a companion when nothing else offered.

When Red set off across the clearing toward the beech woods, Mike paced easily beside him, head up and snuffling prodigiously. Danny had taken the training collar off, and the prospect of another partridge hunt was enticing now that he could run the woods without fear of again becoming entangled. Mike ranged out to trot ahead of his father.

He snuffled warily, then stopped to let Red catch up with him. Just ahead a porcupine was pursuing his wheezy path between two trees. Mike let Red walk in front of him, intending to follow when the older dog led safely around the grunting porky.

Instead, much to Mike's astonishment, Red emitted a happy roar and bounded straight toward it. Rear end in the air, front paws on the ground, he crouched in front of the grunting quill pig and barked. The porcupine thrust his unprotected head between his paws and stopped, presenting a bristling array of spears in all directions.

Mike's amazement increased. Instead of letting well enough alone, Red walked around to the side of the porcupine and thrust an exploring paw toward it. He worked his paw almost to the porcupine's belly, then let out a mighty roar that startled the sluggish animal into walking again.

Red ran beside it, tempting the porcupine to strike with its tail but always keeping just out of reach. He leaped over and around it, turning the beast he was teasing in half a dozen directions before he finally let the worried porcupine climb another tree. The play over, Red snuffled at some more grass.

Mike sat still, too overcome to do anything else. Never before had he looked upon Red as anything extraordinary, or even interesting. But what he had just seen was unheard of, far and away outshining the coyote that had caught the partridge. The fact that he had fearlessly approached a porcupine was enough in itself to make Red supreme.

The worshipful Mike edged close to his father, who ignored him and continued to snuffle at the grass. Mike stayed near, content just to warm himself in the radiance of such a hero. He trotted obediently behind him when Red returned to the clearing.

Danny called both into the cabin and shut the door. Though he had not nearly exhausted his boundless vitality, Mike was satisfied to stay in the cabin as long as Red didn't leave. And the big dog gave no sign of leaving. He sat solemnly next to the stove, watching Danny clean a shotgun. Ross was nowhere in sight.

Red sat so near his beloved master that his furry coat almost touched Danny's arm. His mouth was open and he was panting expectantly. Red had long known from the weather itself that partridge season was in the offing. He knew very well what a shotgun was for, and when Danny started polishing his a partridge hunt could be only hours away. Red could not know, of course, that partridge season opened at high noon of this very day.

Mike, who had never hunted to a gun, attached no significance to Danny's actions. He knew only that great excitement was in the air.

Danny prepared and ate a sandwich, filled his pockets with shotgun shells, and let Red out. Mike sprang happily up, ready and willing to follow, but Danny closed the door and took the training collar from its peg. Mike backed warily. He knew all about such collars, and if he could possibly help it nobody, not even Danny, was ever going to put another one on him. When Danny twitched his fingers, Mike wagged an apologetic tail and refused to come.

Danny spoke, but Mike still had no intention of being caught. When Danny tried to corner him, he crawled under the stove and stayed there. Finally Danny put the collar back on its hook, slammed the door, and left.

Mike crawled from beneath the stove and sat wistfully in front of the door. He felt very forlorn and mistreated, but he still had no intention of wearing the collar; memory of what it could do was still new and fresh. He moaned plaintively, and lay down by the door.

Two hours later Danny and Red came back. Holding no grudges, Mike wagged both back into the cabin. His interest was suddenly alerted. Partridge scent was all about, and grew stronger as it had time to fill the closed cabin. Danny took four partridges from his hunting jacket and put them on the table. Mike edged nearer, and nearer, as though fearful that the birds might fly away. He reared on a chair and looked steadily at them, too fascinated to think of anything else.

When Danny thrust a partridge at him, he was so startled that he leaped backward to the floor. For a moment he stood still, then slowly advanced to take the proffered game. Gently, never ruffling a feather, he closed his jaws on it and sighed blissfully. Never before had he known a moment such as this. When Danny took the partridge away, Mike whined to have it back.

"That's enough," said Danny. "Now you'd better run a bit."

He pushed Red and Mike out the door, and the puppy tried at once to get back in. But the door was tightly shut. Failing to enter the cabin, Mike turned to trot along behind Red. He followed the big dog dutifully, wagging his tail and changing his stride when Red changed his. Red started for the beech woods.

Mike stayed behind, still imitating exactly everything the older dog did. Red had been out only a short while, not nearly long enough to tire himself, and he wanted more hunting. When he caught the scent of a partridge he froze instantly on it.

Mike honored for as long as he could resist the tantalizing smell of the bird. Then he went in to flush, and raced along beneath the disappearing partridge. He lost it just as a tornado struck him.

It was Red, a wrathful Red who had seen all the finer points of partridge hunting violated by an unteachable puppy. He flung himself on Mike, raking with punishing teeth again and again. Mike squealed, and flung himself on his back in token of abject surrender. Snarling, Red stood astride the prostrate puppy. Finally he turned his back and walked away.

Mike slunk behind him. Many things had gone right this day but so many others had gone wrong. It was far too bewildering to understand. The mystified, chastened puppy followed Red at a safe distance.

When they reached the cabin, Mike's nose led him irresistibly around to the refuse heap. He dug a discarded partridge wing from the litter, took it tenderly in his mouth, and carried it into the cabin with him. Mike lay down behind the stove, cradling the wing beneath him.

It was a great comfort.

# 10. Tower Head

Time passed swiftly but the season did not adjust accordingly. Beeches, maples, birches, basswood, and other deciduous trees changed color and the leaves rustled to the earth. But the weather remained warm. Right up to the first week in November, Danny did not find it necessary to change his light leather hunting jacket for a heavier woolen one.

It was a freak year, Ross said, but because it was so uncertain, it was due to change swiftly when it changed. Overnight they were going to have howling winter, and one that would last until late spring. Nor could Ross be shaken in that idea despite the weather's continued mildness. You didn't see green grass in November, he maintained, without also seeing snow in May.

Danny fretted because furs were not yet prime; the big snowshoe hares whose change of color told trappers when they could profitably start stringing trap lines had not yet undergone the complete change from brown to white. Some of them did present a ludicrous pinto effect, half white and half brown.

They could take bounty furs, and Danny and Ross ran their trap lines steadily. There were now thirty-one weasels, eleven gray foxes, and three big-footed wildcats, in the shed behind the house. That was almost a hundred and fifty dollars in bounty fur alone, but Danny and Ross had put in so many hours getting it that their pay per hour averaged less than fifty cents. They'd have to do a whole lot better than that if they were going to buy a suitable mate for Red. A good bitch could be had reasonably, but Danny made up his mind to have the best.

Danny had almost given up hope of making anything out of Mike, so when he could spare time from his bounty lines he hunted partridges with Red alone. They were very plentiful, almost at their peak cycle, and he shot as many as the law allowed. The grouse that they couldn't eat at once were canned.

Ross's line of bounty traps was not as long as Danny's nor did he stay out as many hours. There was no doubt about it; Ross was getting too old to run the woods as he formerly had. The lion's share of the hardest work therefore rested on Danny's shoulders.

Never a shotgun enthusiast, but one who relied on his rifle, Ross had taken to using a shotgun only since he had acquired an interest in Irish setters. Now he carried one when making the rounds of his trap lines, and usually took Mike with him.

The first few trips he brought in nothing, then he came in with a limit shoot of five. Without speaking he took them out of his hunting jacket and laid them on the table. Danny glanced inquiringly around at Mike, who sat on his haunches looking up at the table. The red puppy was quivering with excitement.

"Don't tell me he got 'em for you?" Danny asked.

"No," Ross admitted. "No, he didn't. I ran into a whole flock of 'em, so thick I could have got some with a club. Mike wasn't even with me. He's as wild and bull-headed as ever; I'll bet he's chased five thousand grouse out of range."

Ross looked at the anxious puppy, then at Danny.

"Danny, that pup's got everything except some one thing. If he was a horse, he'd take apples and sugar out of your hand, then pitch you fifteen feet the first time you got on his back. But he's not an outlaw. He lives for bird huntin', but he aims to hunt his own way. Try to club or beat it out of him and you'll ruin him entire. I can't help wonderin' if I was wrong about him. I don't know if he'll ever come around."

Danny said nothing. He had thought from the first that Mike was worthless, but hadn't wanted to hurt Ross by saying so.

"Sure wish I was smarter than I am," Ross said, "and knew what to do with the mutt."

"Want to take him back?" Danny asked.

Ross grinned and shook his head. "We'll keep him around a while. Once, before you were born, I had a big black hound almost as bull-headed as Mike. When he wanted to hunt he hunted—in his own way. Then one day he came around."

"How?" Danny inquired.

"He tangled with a lashin' big lynx and was gettin' his ears chewed off when I came along and shot the lynx. That showed him he was wearin' pants too big for him, and that it took two of us to make a go of huntin'. Somethin' like that ought to happen to Mike, to make him want to hunt for us instead of just for himself."

"Maybe," Danny was dubious.

He put their dinner of roast partridge, mashed potatoes, creamed carrots, and scalding coffee, on the table. They ate in silence, did the few chores there were, and went to bed.

Though he was usually asleep a few seconds after his head hit the pillow, tonight Danny was wakeful. He wanted to work with dogs, and not be just a trapper. Had they made a mistake in leaving their job? Perhaps, when Mr. Haggin returned, he would set everything right again. It was going to take longer than Danny had thought to buy a mate, and meanwhile all they had was Red and Mike. Crippled as he was, Red was still a good gun dog but he could never win any field trials. Mike was just plain useless. The only thing left to do was hump himself and get that mate for Red.

Up with dawn, Danny ran his bounty traps over the beech ridges and took two more weasels. His first trip over the same line had produced eight. Weasels were getting scarce; he would have to pull his traps. It would not do to exterminate them. Even bloody killers like weasels had their place in checking over-populations of mice, moles, and other vermin. As he went on, Danny picked up eleven of his weasel traps.

Red snapped to a point. Danny dropped his traps and edged up behind the big dog. He went in to flush, but the single partridge that rose was a wary bird that kept trees between the gunner and himself. Danny missed, grinned, and slipped another shell into his gun. Red looked reproachfully at him.

"Got to miss some," Danny defended himself. "You needn't look at me that way, Red. Go hunt up another bird."

Red trotted on, and a snowshoe rabbit jumped up in his path. Danny watched the big hare bob out of sight. It was almost white, so Danny made his decision. Within a week he could start trapping some of the more valuable fur-bearers. Mink, fairly good now, should be prime then. But before he did any serious trapping he wanted to go back to Tower Head and investigate the marten he had seen there. There might be several of them, and if so he might get almost enough fur to buy the dog he must have.

Danny swung back on his line and started picking up more traps. They were number ones and would be used for mink later on, so he dumped them into a hollow stump. When he gathered some larger traps, with a bigger jaw spread, he put them into his pack. These he would take to Tower Head and use for the marten.

Red pointed again and Danny edged in behind him. Two partridges thundered up and Danny dropped the nearer bird with his right barrel. He swung on the other with his left, and watched it tumble to the ground when he shot. Red rambled out to retrieve. He brought the first bird back to Danny, then got the second. Danny pocketed both.

"There," he sniffed. "Maybe that'll give you

some different notions about me. How many hunters you ever been out with that can make a double on grouse?"

Red wagged his tail and Danny grinned as he continued back over his line. Taking only the bigger traps, he hung the rest from trees or cached them in hollow stumps. He would pick them up when he was ready to use them and traps left to weather in the woods were always better anyhow. If they were left around the cabin they would be certain to pick up human scent.

Just before nightfall, with five partridges in his pockets and fourteen traps in his pack, Danny reached the cabin. He put his pack down outside, but carried the partridges in and laid them on the table. Ross looked disinterestedly at them.

"Don't you think we got enough pa'tridges, boy? I've eaten so many they're comin' out of my ears."

"I reckon we got enough. Anyhow, we'll have to quit hunting them in a few days. The snowshoes are almost turned. Pretty soon we can really lay traps."

"Good! I've sort of been achin' to get after the mink and otter. Might take a few foxes too, though they aren't worth what they were. I remember the time when you got fifteen dollars for a good prime red."

"Lucky to get that for a silver, now. I took only weasels today, Pappy, and I looked at every trap."

"Time we laid off, then. Did you pull your traps?"

Danny nodded. "Cached most of 'em, but there's fourteen ones and a half in my pack."

"What you aim to do with those?"

Danny hesitated. If there were enough marten on Tower Head, it would be a rich strike. If there weren't, it would mean only that Ross's hopes would be built up and dashed down. Besides, it was a long, hard climb up there and Ross was in no condition for it.

"Thought I might slide up onto Stoney Lonesome and see what's there. I'll take the traps with me in case I find anything. Figure on laying out a couple of nights, so I'll pack blankets and grub."

"If you're goin' to lay out on Stoney Lonesome you'd best watch yourself."

"There's nothing up there that can hurt me."

"I don't mean varmints. But this weather we've been havin' is due to shift. Mark my words. You goin' to take Red with you?"

Danny shook his head and thought fast. The Tower Head climb would be pretty hard for Red. But his father thought he was going to Stoney Lonesome, Red could make that easily, and Ross knew it.

"Think I'll take Mike," Danny said. "May get a chance to do something with him, and being out a lot might teach him some sense." He hoped his reason sounded convincing.

"Good idea," Ross agreed. "Mike's good company, and he might learn somethin' at that."

That night Danny laid out his pack. He put in two woolen blankets that would keep him warm no matter how much the weather changed, a two day's supply of food for himself and Mike, and plenty of water-proofed matches. Since he was carrying his own food, and would not have to get any,

he decided to pack his .22 revolver rather than a
heavier, clumsier shotgun or rifle.

Danny was up, as usual, at dawn. He fed himself
and Mike, shouldered the pack, and said goodbye to
Ross. At Danny's order, Red reluctantly went back
to his rug and lay down. Mike raced happily into the
dimly lighted morning and at once was off on a
wild gambol across the clearing. Mike was wild and
bull-headed, but he would follow Danny. In fact,
unless he was tied or penned, he could not be prevented from following. Danny started up the trail.

A half hour later Mike careened crazily up behind
him, made a sudden stop that almost tumbled him
on his black nose, frisked around Danny for a few
minutes, and was away again. Danny grinned
faintly. Mike was useless, but he had a contagious
enthusiasm. It was impossible to dislike or resent
him.

Swinging on with a mile-eating woodsman's
stride, Danny began to climb. He paid no attention
to Mike, who came and went as he pleased but at
least had enough woods sense to find Danny at any
time he wished.

"Hi," Danny greeted, when Mike caught up with
him again. "Come back to walk with me for a spell,
eh? I'm real flattered."

Mike, who had had enough of running for the
time being, tagged amiably behind. Danny buttoned his jacket and wished he had a heavier one.

Summer might reign in Budgegummon, but up
here on Tower Head's slope autumn had arrived
with full force. The beeches and other hardwoods

were completely bare of leaves. Through the empty branches a bitter wind lashed at Danny. He bent his head to the wind and kept on. He would not get too cold as long as he stayed on the move, and the two woolen blankets in his pack would provide ample warmth for sleeping even in zero weather. It was not likely to become as cold as that for a long while.

Mike, who had been hugging Danny's heels for the past fifteen minutes, whined uneasily. Danny turned to him.

"You got the shivers too? What's the matter with everything today?"

As they went on, Danny became more alert. It was about here that he had seen the first marten. If there was good hunting in the vicinity, it might have remained near. Danny swerved from the trail into the beech forest.

He kept his head tilted, studying the trees. High in a big beech he caught a flash of gray, and saw a squirrel creeping along a branch. Suddenly it began to run, flung itself onto another branch, ran up the tree, and dived into a hole. Then he saw another squirrel. Danny felt a little disappointment. If there were many marten here, there should not be so many squirrels.

Danny swung out of the woods and back to the deer path he had followed this far. He rubbed numbed hands together and walked briskly to warm himself. It was very cold, and the wind had sharpened.

Mike left him for another hunt, and Danny let

him go. The red puppy would come back when he felt like it, and even Mike could not get into much trouble on Tower Head. Danny went on.

An hour later he knew. There was almost certainly only a single pair of marten on Tower Head, therefore his hopes of wealth from that source must be put aside. Since he had accomplished what he had set out to do, he might as well go back to Budgegummon. His bunk there would be a lot more comfortable than a pair of blankets on top of this inhospitable mountain. Danny swung around.

As he did so, he was struck in the face by a cold rush of air that sent him reeling. Winter had struck at last, and without warning. Danny gasped his spent breath back in and hurried on, looking for Mike.

In a matter of minutes, the wind's moaning whine became a mighty roaring. A beech tree nearby snapped four feet above the trunk and fell, carrying smaller trees with it. Danny stopped in his tracks. All about, the great beeches were bending and groaning as the wind lashed them. He was in a serious situation and knew it.

Now he understood the movement of the herd of deer he had witnessed this morning. The deer had been going down from Tower Head not because they wanted to wander but because, in their own mysterious way, they had known the storm was coming. Ross would have known why they were on the march, but Danny hadn't guessed.

At one side, a mighty bough broke from a tree and fell, leaving a ragged scar and a long piece of bark dangling like a strip of skin. The wounded tree seemed to shiver.

Danny picked his way among the storm-shaken trees, trying to watch them and still keep an eye out for Mike. He walked slowly, eyes and ears alert. To rush into this holocaust would mean certain doom. He side-stepped nimbly as a tree directly in his path went down. He walked on.

Then, behind him, a great limb cracked loose from its mother trunk and swung forward. Danny had a split second in which to dodge, but the limb had fallen too suddenly and with too little warning.

It struck Danny's head and he fell face down.

# 11. White Prison

Danny stirred, and fought sluggishly to a bewildered awakening. For a few minutes he lay still, unable to think where he was or what had happened. Bit by bit, like crooked pieces of a jigsaw puzzle, he fitted the picture together.

He was up on Tower Head, he remembered, where he had come to investigate marten sign. Summer had suddenly become winter, and winter had been ushered in by a terrible wind storm which had ripped through the beech trees. Some had broken. Great boughs had been torn like match sticks from their parent trunks, and one had hit him.

Danny lapsed into a numbed slumber and a second time fought to wakefulness. A thousand drums seemed to pound within his aching head and for a moment he felt very sick. The spasm passed, and when it did he could think more clearly. It had, he remembered, been daylight when he decided to return to Budgegummon. Now inky blackness surrounded him. Danny stretched his hand forth and a warm, wet tongue licked it gently. His exploring fingers found Mike's silky coat. At once he felt a tremendous rush of gratitude. Until now he had not remembered bringing Mike.

He sat up, and when he did his head broke through the fresh, fluffy snow that covered him. It had, then, snowed while he lay unconscious and the fact that it had covered him was the reason why he had not frozen to death. That and Mike, for the red puppy had found him, and was crouching as close as he could get to his injured master. Again Danny gratefully stroked the red puppy's fur.

The snow was still falling fast; even in the darkness Danny felt its soft, deadly caress as he stood erect. He stumbled and almost fell, but by a mighty effort stiffened his legs.

He was aware of Mike pressing closely against his feet, and he could see nothing whatever. Overwhelmed by another spasm of illness, and weighed down by an unbearable burden on his back, Danny crouched in the snow and gave himself over to sheer misery. When he recovered he felt better and could think more clearly.

The burden he bore was only his pack, Danny realized, and forced himself to be calm. What had happened? First, winter had struck with savage fury. There had been no snow at all during the afternoon, but now it was up to Danny's knees and still falling. He was in the forest, and therefore the snow would not have drifted much. However, there was no possible way he could get to Budgegummon without crossing open spaces where there would be deep drifts, and he had no snowshoes. Even with every possible bit of good luck, it would take him days just to get off the mountain.

Then he did his best to forget it and give his thoughts to immediate problems. Falling snow had prevented his freezing to death, but he was numb with cold and ached in every muscle. Before he did anything else he must get a fire going.

Danny plowed forward, a step at a time, groping hands stretched out before him. A few feet from where he had started, he stopped to rest. He was panting, and beads of sweat clung to his forehead. As soon as he stopped, the cold attacked again; he licked frost particles from his upper lip. Starting forward again, he stumbled over a snow-covered limb, and fell on his hands and knees. For a moment he rested where he was, too tired to get up. A delicious, soothing warmth enveloped him. Then Mike's questing nose touched his face.

Danny fought his way to a standing position. Now he must keep going or die. The snow would not save him again for he had started to sweat. Should he relax for more than a few seconds the sweat would freeze, and if it did he was all through. Danny forced his numb body forward.

He jarred his shoulder against a standing tree and stopped, raising cold hands to feel the tree. It was small, scarcely a foot through, and ragged wisps of paper-thin bark hung like shedding fur from it. A great hope leaped in Danny.

Solely by accident he had bumped into a birch. The parchment-like bark covering the trunk was as thin as paper and burned as readily. Keeping hold of the tree with one hand, Danny trampled a hole in the snow.

Carefully feeling his way, he stripped handfuls of bark from the tree and put it in the hole he had trampled. Then he knelt down, holding both hands firmly against Mike's warm fur. When circulation returned to his hands, Danny felt in his pocket for the metal match box he always carried. He unscrewed the top, extracted one match, and carefully tightened the cover down. Striking the match against the box's rough side, Danny held the tiny flame against his pile of birch bark. The match died, and almost went out. Danny's hand trembled, and a cold shiver rippled up his spine. Then a corner of bark curled, smoldered, and burst into flame. Almost instantly the whole pile was alight.

Danny's happy shout vied with the softly ominous sound of falling snow and the whine of the wind that sighed through the beech forest. Guiding himself by the fire's light, he turned back to the tree and feverishly groped for the outer tips of small dry twigs that broke easily. He filled his hands with them and went back to throw them on his dying fire. Hungry flames crackled their way into this stronger nourishment. Turning back to the tree, Danny wrenched off an inch-thick limb, broke it into sections, and heaped them on the flames. The fire climbed higher.

Danny gratefully appreciated his good luck in having an ample supply of wood practically within reach of his fire. Very few trees on Tower Head were dead, and chance alone had guided him to one of them. Fuel awaited only the taking.

He broke off more and bigger branches and carried them to his fire. He laid them the long way, pushing them farther up as the ends burned, and arranged a layer of dead sticks to sit on. There were blankets in his pack, but Danny was too tired to try making a proper bed. Heat from the fire melted an increasing circle of snow, and Danny changed his seat.

Mike, for once subdued, crouched down beside him. Danny put a hand on the red puppy's ruff and drew him close. Mike had already atoned for all his past sins merely by providing company. Danny spoke softly to him.

"Tomorrow we'll see about getting out of here, pup. Sure wish I had a pair of snowshoes."

As soon as he had spoken, Danny wished that he had not even thought about what tomorrow would bring. Certainly there was no immediate hope of rescue for he had told Ross that he was going up Stoney Lonesome. Ross would not worry unduly for a couple of days, and if he did start out, it would not be toward Tower Head. If they were going to be helped, Danny and Mike would have to help themselves.

Danny gazed soberly into the fire. It was ordinarily a few hours' walk back to Budgegummon. Now deep snow covered every inch of the way, and progress would be painfully slow. It would take several days to reach Budgegummon, or even to get down into one of the sheltered valleys where, Danny hoped, the snow would not be so deep.

He knew he was in serious trouble, but bewailing the fact, or worrying about what might happen, would not help at all. Tonight, certainly, he could do nothing except sit here by the fire. He pushed a couple of sticks farther up, bent his head forward so that the collar of his jacket came up around his neck, and dozed fitfully. Creeping cold awakened him when the fire burned low, and Danny built it up again.

He was awakened by Mike's warning bark. He jerked erect, one hand stealing to the grip of his .22, but he could see nothing. Mike touched his hand with a cold nose, and Danny lifted his head to find that dawn had come. He stared around in bewilderment.

The once stately forest on Tower Head had become a shambles. Big trees were piled helterskelter, a Gargantuan jumble of jackstraws. Boughs and branches had blown down among them in a litter of kindling. As Danny plodded over to get more wood for his fire, he thought of the food in his pack.

Expecting to be away for only two days, he had not packed much food. There was a little slab of bacon, flour, syrup, a chunk of meat, salt and pepper, and coffee. There was not nearly enough of anything. Bucking deep snow would require effort and burn up energy fast. The food that Danny had would have to be conserved to the utmost.

Reluctantly he unbuckled the straps that closed his pack and took out the package of flour. He sliced four strips of bacon from his small chunk and put them into the skillet. Melting snow in the coffee pot, he mixed flapjack batter, and pushed the sizzling bacon to one side of the skillet. He poured a flapjack and let it cook. When it was finished he gave it to Mike, along with two strips of bacon.

The red puppy wagged his appreciation, and gulped his food. He looked on with great interest as Danny fixed the same amount for himself. Mike licked his chops eagerly, and begged with limpid eyes. Danny looked at him.

"Nix," he said. "We're on short rations until we find something else. If one of us eats then both of us will, and there'll be no stealing from each other."

Danny washed the coffee pot with more melted snow and brewed coffee. Letting it cool a little, he drank it directly from the pot. Then he brushed snow over the fire, buckled his pack on, and stood for a moment as he tried to pick out a route through the fallen trees.

Danny plunged his foot into deep snow, and almost collapsed as a red-hot iron seemed to flash across his right side. He felt a momentary dizziness, then eased back into his tracks.

Obviously he was hurt more than he knew. He had not felt it last night either because he was partly dazed or because his injury had not had time to stiffen. Possibly he had a couple of broken ribs or internal injuries. Still, there was no one to help him. What was to be done, he must do alone. Days might elapse before anyone thought of looking for him on Tower Head. Danny tried another experimental step, this time with his left foot.

He stepped into deep snow and brought his right foot up. Danny gritted his teeth. The pain was there, but it was not as intense as when he had tried to walk with his right foot forward. He plowed ahead, favoring his right side as much as possible. He had to keep on.

Mike plodded along in the trail Danny broke, the

top of his head four inches below the snow line.
The red puppy's eyes were anxious, and he whined
at intervals. He was worried, but had every faith in
the man he was following.

Danny stopped to rest, leaning against a tree to
ease the burden on his back. When he cast his eye
over the trail he had made he was panicky. He must
have been on the move for half an hour, yet last
night's camp was no more than a stone's throw
away. He was making very poor time.

It was impossible to go any faster in his condition.
He was already panting from exertion. It was turning warmer, too, he noticed. The snow was stopping
and the clouds overhead were breaking. A slanting
ray of warm sun stole down; the soft snow would
soon begin to melt. Danny unbuttoned his jacket,
pushed his knitted cap back on his head, and went
on.

Two hours later the top of the snow was a soggy
mess. Dark wet patches appeared here and there,
dips and hollows in what had been a perfectly
smooth blanket. Hard to buck before, now the set-
tling snow became doubly difficult to wade through.
Danny stopped again to rest.

Hunger that would not be subdued arose within
him. Danny licked his lips, and tried not to think of
the food in his pack. But he could not help thinking
of it, and the very fact that he had food within reach
seemed to induce a strange weakness. Danny
turned to look at Mike, who was sitting in the snow
looking expectantly up at him. Again Danny licked
his lips.

The proper course, he had always heard, was to
hoard every scrap of food when one had little. But,
even though he had come only a short distance, he
had burned a terrific amount of energy doing it. It
was impossible to continue without eating; he
would just have to take a chance of getting some
sort of food later on.

Danny stopped and cooked more of his scanty
supplies, dividing them equally with Mike. When
he had eaten he felt better, but by then it was even
more difficult to travel through the wet snow. Every
foot he advanced was a foot that had to be fought
for, and every step cost pain. He tried counting his
steps, then gave it up. The *next* step was the thing.
It was all-important, and if he could make that one
he could also make the one to follow. Every step he
took carried him that much nearer Budgegummon
and that much farther away from Tower Head. Distance lost its meaning because of the effort it cost
to make that all-important next step.

The sun went down and Danny buttoned his
jacket, for with the approach of twilight the cold
returned. He stopped to wipe the sweat from his
forehead, and considered. He had to rest, for if he
tried going on through the darkness he would only
exhaust himself and probably fall. Danny glanced at
Mike, who sat in the snow, ears erect and tail flat
behind him. He whined apprehensively and Danny
made up his mind. It was time to camp.

He was very tired, and when he chopped wood
for a fire his axe seemed a wooden thing with no
edge at all. Danny stopped twice while he was

chopping to look at the pile of wood, then wearily turned to cut more. Finally he scooped the snow away, built a fire, laid a mat of twigs, and put one blanket on it. The other he laid on top, and made a pillow with his pack. Mike crowded close to him, and Danny stroked the red puppy's ears.

"Poor pup," he soothed. "You sure got in a fix when you went out with me, didn't you?"

As he comforted Mike, a sudden relief overcame Danny himself. It had been a terrible, endless day. But it had ended, and not until tomorrow must he resume fighting his way through the snow. Tomorrow was a long while away, and they were in camp. At least for the moment their troubles were ended, and within itself that was a relief. The moment was the thing and the future he could work out. Danny prodded the pack with his foot.

"We got this far," he told Mike. "Let's celebrate."

Danny dived recklessly into his store of food and prepared a filling meal for Mike and himself. After eating, he drowsed in front of the fire, then crawled into his blankets. Ordinarily it would have been a hard bed, but not tonight. Danny dropped at once into a deep and untroubled sleep from which he did not awaken until dawn had again come.

He sat up to look at his dead fire. During the night Mike had become cold, and had crawled underneath the blankets to take advantage of the warmth offered by Danny. Now he tumbled unwillingly out of his comfortable sleeping place, stretching and yawning. Danny looked at him and felt comforted just from the puppy's presence.

Yesterday had been a sick day. Still suffering from the effects of the blow when the branch had struck him, Danny had done what he could do. This morning, after a good night's sleep, he could look at their predicament sanely. They were still trapped in a white prison from which there was scant hope of escape, but they must get out if they were to live. It was that simple.

Methodically Danny set about the preparation of a scanty breakfast. He divided the food exactly in half, fed the red puppy and himself. Then he gathered his blankets, shouldered his pack, and started off. After two steps he stopped and looked down at the snow in dismay.

During the night it had turned much colder, and a crust had formed on top of the soggy snow. Mike, climbing up, could run about on it at will. But at every step Danny's foot broke the brittle crust. He shivered, then plodded doggedly ahead.

Mike skipped happily about on the crust, no longer finding it necessary to plod in his master's trail. Danny kept envious eyes on the puppy. If there was some way to make him go there, Mike could reach Budgegummon by nightfall. If Mike came in alone, Ross would set out at once to find Danny. Then he shook his head in despair; it would be hopeless to try to make the obstinate puppy return to the cabin. If only Red were with him!

Mike stopped suddenly, and froze in his tracks. For a moment Danny forgot to breathe; Mike was on partridges! Danny's hand slid to the grip of his .22 revolver.

"Whoa, Mike!" he said tensely. "Whoa!"

Intently he searched the little scattering of evergreens at which Mike was pointing. Partridges were hard to see, but if he could catch one on the ground he had a chance of getting it.

Then Mike went in to flush. There was a thunder of wings and Danny saw five partridges rise. He shot at them, pulling the trigger time after time as he sent the little leaden pellets flying after the grouse. But he knew it was hopeless.

Mike dashed out of sight, and Danny looked after him with sick eyes.

# 12. A Rebel's Heart

Trying to keep the partridges in sight, Mike raced happily across the frozen crust. He slipped, went down, and rolled into a small tree. Mike picked himself up and looked about for the birds he had flushed. They were gone, and he could neither see nor smell them. The puppy sat down to puzzle out their probable whereabouts. Then he started toward a copse of evergreens. Halfway there he turned and looked back at Danny. Never before, when partridges were near, had he let anything interfere with their pursuit. But never before had he found himself in a situation such as this one. What should he do?

When the great wind storm had struck, Mike, unlike Danny, had not tried to make his way through it. Instead, the red puppy had curled at the base of a great boulder and waited there, shivering as the mighty beeches trembled and crashed all around him. When the wind died, Mike had started out at once to reach Danny. He had found him before the snow started, lying motionless where he had fallen. The red puppy, sensing something wrong, had tried to awaken Danny by whining, then by pawing, and when he could get no response had curled up beside him. Even though Mike, the rebel, acknowledged no master, the age-old bond be-

tween dog and man had instinctively kept him by
Danny's side in time of trouble.

So Mike hesitated now, instead of rushing after
the partridges, because he knew that Danny was
still in trouble. There was an urgency in the way
Danny plodded on, and a tense desperation, both
of which were entirely foreign to any normal state.

The red puppy turned halfway around to go back.
But the will to hunt, as powerful as it had ever
been, held him where he was. Mike trembled uncertainly, pulled in two directions at once and
wholly undecided as to what he had better do. Then
the lure of the hunt prevailed, and he started toward
the evergreens.

Because he was certain his game had gone into
them, he did not bother to swing downwind where
he could get a better scent. He raced full speed toward his objective, then slowed down as he approached it. Wrinkling his nose to clear it, he
detected the partridges and stiffened in a point.

He did not rush in at once because there was another faint scent, one he had never smelled before,
underlying the odor of partridges. The smell had
something of fear in it, and evil, something Mike
did not like. He did not know what it was and because nothing except the porcupine had ever hurt
him he eased cautiously forward.

The partridges were in the very center of the
thicket, where green branches intertwined so
closely that they were almost impenetrable. Mike
located the birds exactly and flung himself forward.
He heard a partridge's alarmed cluck, and dashed

insanely toward the sound. Then his quarry drummed upward and Mike threw himself to one side after it.

A second later and he would have been too late to avoid the beast that had been in the thicket even before the partridges, the thing Mike had smelled and ignored. It was a snow-bound puma, a tawny, rippling beast almost invisible in the hemlocks.

The puma had stared with hungry eyes at the partridges when they flew into the thicket, but he had not moved a muscle. They alighted a dozen feet away, too far to let him catch one. But he knew himself unseen; if he did not move one or more of the birds might venture within striking distance.

The hungry puma instantly transferred all his attention to Mike when the red puppy entered the thicket. Here was food in plenty, good food; he had eaten a dog before. He waited until Mike seemed near enough, then launched his lithe spring.

However, the puma did not distinguish between dogs and he had previously caught and eaten only an aging, lost hound. Mike was much younger and infinitely more agile. The puma's outstretched claws missed their target by three inches and Mike dodged out of the thicket.

He ran as fast as he could, with healthy fear lending speed to his legs. Mike had never been hurt by anything except the porcupine, but the law of survival was part of his heritage and he knew that the puma intended to kill him. Furthermore, he knew that it could. Mike raced full speed back toward Danny and found him resting wearily in the snow with his pack braced against a dead stump. Mike slid to a halt beside him and turned around to bristle and bark.

He faced the direction from which he had come, testing the wind with his nose, while the hungry puma lingered behind some brush a few hundred feet away. Having caught man scent, the big cat had no wish to come any nearer. Mike barked again, challenging his enemy, and Danny's hand played around the red puppy's ears.

"What's the matter?" Danny asked. "What's up, Mike? You see your own shadow out there?"

Without understanding the words, Mike sensed the comradeship in the tone of voice.

Danny could not know, nor could Mike himself reason out, that a change had been worked within him. The days when he had been only a senseless puppy, with never a thought except for himself, were definitely in the past. Time, and affection, and now shared trouble, were all combining to work the change. Mike was growing up.

Being a dog, neither the past nor the future mattered to him. The moment was the thing, and now Mike sat on the crusted snow reading the wind that told him of the puma's movements. The big cat had made a circle and gone to one side. Now he lay behind a fallen beech, eyes and ears alert and tail twitching as he studied the situation. The puma had no desire to expose himself to a man, but neither did he have the slightest intention of abandoning the trail until he had caught Mike. Cunning and wise, he would follow the pair until he found an opportunity to catch and kill the dog.

Mike growled low in his throat, and Danny looked questioningly in the direction the red puppy was looking, then turned to go on. Mike stayed behind him, making short little excursions out on the crust to read the wind to better advantage. The puma was coming, slinking along their trail like a tawny shadow. But so woods-wise was he that he never once showed himself. Mike knew he was coming only because his nose told him.

With only a mouthful of cold food at noon, they plodded slowly on. The sun started its downward sweep and with its descent the cold became more intense. Accustomed to being outside, and provided by nature with a suitable coat for all seasons, Mike did not feel it. Danny tried to tighten his jacket and shivered as he stopped in a cluster of big beech trees.

A squirrel chattered in one of the beeches. Mike glanced disinterestedly up, not caring about such game. It was fun to chase squirrels, and to watch them leap with panicky haste into the trees. That was all. But now Mike sensed the change in Danny.

Dead-tired and almost apathetic for the past hour, Danny was now tensely alert. The revolver in his hand, he stood in his tracks and looked eagerly into the towering trees. Nothing happened; the squirrel did not even chatter again. Mike knew what Danny did not, that it had gone into a hole in one of the trunks, but long after the squirrel had found safety Danny continued to stare up into the trees.

Then, with a despairing little gesture, he sheathed his gun and set about gathering firewood. Mike crowded anxiously in, staying as close to Danny as he could get and risking a burned nose when Danny lighted a match with which to start his fire. An eddying breeze brought him the puma's scent. It had come in very close, but when smoke started curling from the fire it retreated. The ravenous cat was not so desperately hungry that he would risk getting near a fire. Mike followed the puma's progress with his nose. He also watched Danny's preparation of their meager meal.

The red puppy had never wondered about the source of his food. He knew only that humans had never let him go hungry. When his belly was empty, they gave him something to fill it and he was sure that it would be filled now. Mike gobbled the tiny piece of meat and the bit of bread Danny gave him, and looked questioningly about for more. He whined when Danny ate an equal amount and sat staring dully into the fire. The red puppy scraped his master's arm with an impatient paw. Danny stirred angrily.

"There's no more!" he half shouted. "See?"

Mike sniffed distantly at the pack when Danny opened it for him. He flattened his ears and rolled appeasing eyes, not understanding the fact that food supplies were practically gone and uncomfortable because he was still hungry. Mike knew only that, for some unaccountable reason, Danny was angry with him and he did not like it.

He retreated to the edge of the light circle cast by the fire, then came back within it, for his nose told him that the hungry puma still lingered in the shadows. It was no place for him. In the semi-darkness, he moved confidently closer to Danny. His paws twitched.

He was hungry, but neither exhausted nor terrified. Mike knew that he had been near death when he met the puma, but now that he was again with Danny, that threat was removed. Today, for the first time, he had learned that he was not self-sufficient, but part of a team. He moved softly over to be nearer Danny, and stared steadily into the unfriendly night.

The puma was creeping nearer. A weak moon had risen, casting moving shadows across the snow, and the puma was taking advantage of them to get nearer the camp. He felt bolder now, for the fire sent up only straggling wisps of smoke. Wrapped in his blankets, Danny had surrendered to exhaustion. Mike snuffled again at the creeping puma, then edged in until his rear paws were braced against the sleeping Danny. There fear left him. Alone he could do little, but together he and Danny could face any threat.

The red puppy growled harshly, and the advancing puma stopped. Then he came on, slowly and furtively. Mike growled again, fiercely this time. The numbed Danny stirred fretfully in his blankets.

The puma was very near now; a little more and he would be within leaping distance. Mike snarled again, and again, as he made ready to repel the attacker. Danny stirred, rolled over, and woke up.

He did not make any noise or cry out when he came awake because he had been born to the woods and wild places. He knew the value of silence, and even sick exhaustion could not make him forget it. When Danny rolled out of his blankets he did so carefully and silently. He inched himself to a sitting position and drew the .22 from its holster.

Mike pricked up his ears and stared intently at a motionless shadow. He knew the puma was there for his nose told him, but he could not be certain he saw it. Danny fixed his eyes on the place, like a hundred other shadows but still unlike any of them. Moving ever so slowly, Danny raised the .22 and squeezed the trigger.

When the little revolver snapped, the shadow melted into the night. The puma, taken by surprise, had silently backed away. He was not hurt and he did not run, for to run would be to expose himself. When he knew he could no longer be seen, the puma turned and loped away after easier game. He had gambled and lost.

Knowing the enemy vanquished, Mike relaxed. For a few minutes Danny remained in a sitting position, the little revolver in his hand. What had he shot at? Had he really seen anything? In any event, Mike was now quiet, so Danny put more wood on the fire and returned to his blankets. When he did,

Mike lifted a corner with his nose, crawled in beside him, and snuggled up against Danny's back. They did not awaken until dawn had come.

Mike waited hopefully, expectantly, as Danny built up the fire and brewed a pot of coffee. There was nothing else, and Mike tried to stay his rising hunger by licking his chops. He snuffled at the steaming coffee, then turned his nose away.

When Danny resumed his heartbreakingly slow progress toward the distant valleys, Mike climbed out of the trail he broke to run about on the crust. He liked that better, for in the trail the sharp edges of the broken snow were like glass, and hurt his feet. Mike looked back to see if Danny was coming, then gave all his attention to what lay ahead.

They were crossing a small clearing where blackberry brambles barred their path. Tall weeds had found a rooting in the brambles, and their seeded tops still protruded above the snow. Mike caught the scent of partridges that were eating the seeds, and started toward them. Then he heard Danny's tense voice.

"Whoa! Whoa, Mike!"

The red puppy paused, and looked around. Again he swung his head to drink in the entrancing scent of partridges. He froze into a point.

The old urge was there, the driving impulse to rush furiously upon his game and see if he could overwhelm it. But for the first time something in Danny's voice stopped him. The sound of the familiar command had a new meaning, the end of a long chain of occurrences. Mike was no longer the wild, undisciplined puppy who had escaped from the Haggin estate. A thousand wild chases were behind him, and Red's punishment, and the endless patience and affection offered by Danny and Ross. And fresh in his mind was the realization that he and Danny had faced, and overcome, danger and terror—together. He quivered with eagerness, but held his point.

There was motion in the brambles. One of the partridges thrust a curious head straight up, then sat still. Mike drooled, and tensed his muscles. Before he could move, he heard the snap of Danny's .22.

Utterly bewildered, the red puppy paused. Two partridges thundered away. But another one remained in the brambles, an inert heap of brown feathers. Mike felt an overwhelming flood of excitement; at last his dearest wishes were realized. Everything else was forgotten as he bounded toward the partridge. Mike closed his jaws about the bird, then Danny's voice penetrated his delirious haze.

"Mike. Come here, Mike."

The puppy stood still, not knowing in this joyful moment just what he should do. Again he heard Danny's voice.

"Fetch, Mike."

Then, at long last, Mike gave his whole heart to a master. He started back toward Danny.

Two days later, well down in a sheltered valley, Mike pricked up his ears and looked at the snow-bound trees ahead of them. He barked, then started happily forward. Danny's incredulous eyes followed him. A moment later Big Red burst out of the trees. A little way behind him was Ross, on snowshoes and pulling a toboggan.

"Danny!" Ross's voice broke. "Boy, I'm right glad to see you!"

"I'm kind of glad to see you," Danny admitted. "What brought you up here?"

"That Red dog," said Ross. "We looked every other place we could think of, and Red wanted to come up here. I figured I might as well follow him. What happened? You hurt bad?"

"Well," Danny said lamely, "I went up Tower Head to look for marten, only there weren't any, and then a big windstorm came, and a limb hit me, and—"

"Save it," Ross commanded. "Climb aboard."

Danny settled gratefully on the toboggan and let Ross wrap him in warm blankets. He fought the drowsiness that overcame him, for he had a very important message. It had nothing to do with marten, or money, or broken ribs. It was something far more important. He fingered the two partridges at his belt.

"We've got a partridge dog, Pappy." Then he fell asleep.

# 13. Trial by Hunting

Danny, his right side strapped, fretted about the cabin. It had been this way for two weeks now, ever since he and Mike had escaped from Tower Head. Two ribs were cracked, the doctor at Centerville had said when Ross took him there on the toboggan. Had he had immediate attention everything would have been simple. But the long struggle through crusted snow had done much to aggravate his condition and the best possible cure would be at least two weeks in the hospital. Overriding Ross's protest, Danny had refused to spend even two days in the hospital. That cost a lot of money which they could not afford.

The pain in his side was bearable as long as he restricted himself to moderate exertion, but he could travel neither far nor fast. He would hit no more long trails this winter. Danny worried. If he and Ross were to get a mate for Red, they must take fur and a lot of it. But if neither could branch into the deep wilderness they were necessarily confined to whatever they could find near home. Danny stooped to pet Red's ears.

"You old mooch hound," he said. "I still don't think there'll ever be a better dog, but that son of yours is almost as good a hunter as you are."

He smiled as he spoke. Mike, as he knew when he was honest with himself, was already an even better hunter than the crippled Red. But he was still not their dog.

Danny glanced impatiently out the window. A fox had been crossing the clearing every third or fourth night. Anxious for as much fur as he could get, Danny had set a couple of traps. But so far nothing had been caught. Danny paced about the cabin, then went outside to the wood pile.

He stooped to gather an armful of wood, then let most of it tumble back into the snow as searing pain wrenched his side. Danny grimaced, then knelt to catch up a couple of pieces of wood. He carried them into the cabin and went back for two more pieces.

The wood box filled slowly, but Danny carried stick after stick until it was completely filled. It was not much, but it was something to do and anything that relieved the endless monotony of just sitting around the cabin was welcome. As usual, Ross and Mike had departed early in the morning to run a line of mink traps, and would not be back until dark.

Danny went into the root cellar for a panful of potatoes, and cut pork chops.

They had plenty of food, but not in great variety, and were getting tired of the same diet. Even Ross's hunter's stews were beginning to taste suspiciously the same.

An hour before twilight, Red raised his head and barked sharply. Going to the door, Danny saw Ross and Mike coming across the clearing. The red puppy skipped gaily ahead and wagged his way into the cabin. He sniffed hungrily at the pork chops.

Danny threw him one. "Here you are, pup. I know you must be starving on account you're always starving."

Danny looked fondly at him, and realized that it was only a short time ago that he had considered Mike a worthless mutt, no good for anything at all. But since the experience on Tower Head, Mike had freely given his heart to Danny and Ross, and now under Ross's magic direction he had developed faster in two weeks than most dogs did in a year. Winning the dog had been hard; teaching him was easy. Mike worked because he loved his masters, not because he feared them. It made a great difference.

Ross came in and took a partridge out of his hunting coat. Danny snorted distastefully.

"I had to get one for him," Ross defended. "Else he won't keep his mind on huntin'."

"Well, I hope you aim to eat it. I had enough of 'em on Tower Head to last me until next year."

"I'll eat it," Ross sniffed, "seein' as you're too high and mighty to sink your teeth into the best grub there is. Anyhow the season ends tomorrow."

"That's good."

Ross sank wearily into a chair. "My tail's a-draggin', boy. Must be gettin' old."

"At least you're not a cripple like me," Danny said.

About to say something else, he busied himself at

the stove. Certainly they wouldn't accomplish their objective this year because neither one could work hard enough. Danny turned the sizzling pork chops in their skillet, then turned to Ross.

"Pappy, do you ever miss Sheilah and the rest of the pups?"

Ross was startled. "Why?"

"Oh, I don't know. It's always seemed to me that rightfully they were at least part our dogs and that we had the start we wanted with them. I bet John Price isn't giving them any kind of a break, and all of them could have amounted to something. Look what Mike did. I know there's nothing we can do, but I think lots about those pups. Wish we'd been able to keep 'em."

Ross spoke slowly. "Sure, I miss 'em, Danny. Only, bein' older than you, I've seen a lot of things I couldn't live without slip through my fingers. We'll just have to start all over again, and we've got Red to start with. Maybe, if Mr. Haggin don't want him, we'll have Mike, too."

Danny said no more, nor did he mention the subject again as the long winter days passed slowly. He missed the deer hunting, but Ross got a nice buck and venison varied their diet. Then, as Christmas came and went, Danny got back on the trap lines.

He could not go far; a couple of miles a day was his limit. But with painstaking thoroughness he worked within a two-mile radius of the cabin. He did not, nor had he expected to, take much fur because such a territory was too small. But he did the best he could.

Then came the spring trapping. They were able to take a few muskrats and their legal quota of four beaver each, but all the fur in their cache would scarcely provide a meager living throughout the summer months. They had gained nothing.

The snow melted, and snow water filled all creek banks to roaring fullness. Even the big drifts in the heights started to rot away. Green grass appeared, and the world was suddenly bursting into spring.

Danny pulled the last of his traps and snares. He was stowing them in the shed when Red and Mike started barking. It was a sharp, challenging sound; someone was coming. Danny went out of the shed to see a rider on a big black horse entering the clearing.

"Mr. Haggin!"

Danny stood still, mouth agape. Mr. Haggin reined his black thoroughbred to a halt and slid from the saddle with practiced ease. Leading his mount, he came forward with hand outstretched.

"Hello, Danny."

"Gee! I'm glad to see you back!"

"It's good to be back," Mr. Haggin smiled. "I've covered a lot of the world in the past few months without finding anything I like better than the Wintapi."

Mike, having decided that he could not bluff this stranger, stopped barking and wagged forward to snuffle. He went from Mr. Haggin to the horse, who bent an inquisitive muzzle to Mike's. Mr. Haggin looked at the puppy with uncommunicative eyes. Danny felt suddenly uncomfortable.

"That's Mike," he said defensively. "He's one of Sheilah's pups. The runt."

"I know."

Danny fumbled for more words, caught in an awkward situation and not knowing just what he should do about it. He was saved by Ross's appearance at the cabin door. Mr. Haggin swung toward Danny's father.

"Hello, you old ridge-runner."

"Hi, Mr. Haggin."

They met and shook hands, two men who were worlds apart in everything save deep-rooted friendship. Mr. Haggin looped his horse's reins about the porch rail, and the restive black stamped his feet and snorted.

"Come on in," Ross invited. "How'd you know we were here?"

"Curley told me where to find you."

They went into the cabin. Danny took a stance near the stove, and said nothing. Red sidled up against his legs and Danny tickled the big dog's ears.

"Why did you two walk out on me?" Mr. Haggin said challengingly.

"Wasn't you we walked out on," Ross said. 'We quit on John Price."

"I was depending on both of you."

Anger underlined Ross's words. "You got Danny and me to handle your Irish setters. We got plumb sick of shovellin' cedar shavin's, cleanin' kennels, and nothin' else."

"Somebody has to do it."

"We would have done it," Danny put in, "but we didn't aim to stand by while Joe Williams ruined Sheilah's pups."

"I tried to explain to you before I left that part of your job was to make my nephew and his trainer understand Irish setters."

"We weren't in charge," Danny replied stubbornly. "We were just told what to do."

Mr. Haggin sighed. "Maybe you've got something," he admitted. "John did sort of take things into his own hands. Among other things, he tore down your old cabin and built a hunting lodge which we need about like we need the colic. To say one thing for him, he built a good lodge while he was about it. Want to live there again?"

Danny and Ross looked at each other. Ross asked the question that was on both their tongues.

"With Sheilah and the pups?"

Mr. Haggin's face clouded. He got up to walk around the cabin. When he spoke, his tone was decisive.

"Look here. You two know my position, but I'll review it. I bought this Wintapi estate with one major purpose in mind. I thought that, among all of us, we could breed and train fine animals. I tried to start with the finest, and if possible wanted to improve them.

"As for dogs, I started with Irish setters because I thought they were the best. But I kept an open mind, and I'm guided by what I see. I'm switching to English setters. John has one pup there that'll be a world-beater. Joe Williams says he'll be ready for the National Field Trials in a couple of years, and he's almost certain to win on the bench too. Now what I want both of you to do is to keep promising hunters up at your old place—I'll build kennels—and train them. But you'll have to work closely with Joe Williams. What do you say?"

Danny glanced questioningly at his father, who turned his eyes away. When Ross spoke, it was to Mr. Haggin.

"Speakin' for myself, and only for myself, the answer is no."

"Why?"

"I'll tell you why. For a long while I thought hounds couldn't be beat. I didn't put any stock in Irish setters when Danny fetched Red home. I was glad because the boy had found somethin' he liked. Then I began to see. Red was all dog. He fought Old Majesty to a standstill, and he was the only dog in the mountains able to do it. He proved his heart, his brains, and somethin' besides. When Sheilah came, she was 'most as good. Mr. Haggin, I switched from hounds to Irishmen because they was the best dogs. They still are."

Mr. Haggin shook his head. "I've seen proof that English setters are better."

"Well, I ain't!" Ross's voice rang through the cabin. "You say your nephew has a huntin' dog! We've got one too! He's your dog, but he ran away and came to us!" Ross pointed at Mike. "Put 'em together, Mr. Haggin! Let 'em run in the same cover, and see which one finds the most birds. Then tell me you got a better dog!"

"Is this a challenge?"

"That's what it is."

"I'll accept it," said Mr. Haggin quietly. "Where and when?"

"Tomorrow mornin'. Pick your own stretch of beech woods."

"All right, then. Until tomorrow."

Without another word Mr. Haggin mounted his horse and rode away. Danny turned to Ross.

"Think Mike can do it? He might break."

"No, he won't. I told you from the first he's got what it takes. Besides, you didn't see him workin' on pa'tridges when you was laid up with those busted ribs. Wait and see."

At dawn, with Mike on a leash to keep him from overexercising, and Red trailing behind, they left the cabin. For a while Danny walked glumly, full of forebodings. Then, unaccountably, he felt a surge of confidence. Ross always knew what he was doing. Danny laid a companionable hand on his father's shoulder.

"Going again, Pappy."

"That's it, boy. You and me, and Red and Mike. Sort of seems right, don't it?"

"It does that."

The sun was up when they came to the Haggin estate. Curley Jordan grinned at them from the barn.

"Good luck. We know about it."

"Rubbed my best rabbit's foot this mornin'," Ross assured him. "We got all the luck, but thanks anyway."

Mike moved a little closer to Ross when Mr. Haggin, John Price, and Joe Williams came from the big house. Mr. Haggin smiled.

"You fellows all know each other, I guess."

They nodded across the space that separated them, and though it was only a few feet Danny felt that it was a great distance, almost too far to span.

"I'll get Jack," Joe Williams said noncommittally.

He disappeared toward the kennels, and Danny heard Sheilah's delighted bark. She knew Ross was near. Joe Williams came back with the English setter, and Danny's heart sank.

The black and white youngster was a dog of fire, and superbly conditioned. Still, there was a certain air in the way he looked at his trainer, and responded instantly to his every command, that gave Danny a ray of hope. Jack had been trained, at least partly, by force. No matter where he went or what he did, he would always keep a wary eye out for Joe Williams. He could never be completely spontaneous.

Red remained quiet, but Mike strained forward to greet the newcomer. They touched noses, then Ross drew Mike back to him. Mr. Haggin cleared his throat.

"We're going on the ridge right back of the house. Is that all right with you?"

"Sure," Ross said cheerfully.

The trainer leading Mr. Haggin and John Price

next, and Ross and Danny bringing up the rear with Mike and Red, they cut directly across a meadow. Joe Williams stopped at the edge of the budding beech trees.

"There'll be grouse anywhere from here on. Shall we make this a starting point?"

"All right with me," Ross said.

"Now as I get it, the idea is to loose both dogs. The one that finds and points the most birds wins. How about a time limit of two hours?"

"Fair enough," Ross agreed.

"Then unleash your dog."

Ross stooped to unsnap Mike's chain, then grasped the red puppy's collar to hold him back while the trainer loosed his charge. The young English setter, quivering in every fiber and wild to be away, nevertheless waited for the word that released him. Then he streaked into the beeches. Five yards behind, Mike followed.

The two dogs flashed among the trees. Retaining the order in which they had climbed the hill, the men went after them. Suddenly the young English setter stiffened in a point. Mike, still running behind, honored instantly.

Danny felt a warm glow of pride. Instead of flushing, and chasing the flushed bird, Mike remained steady as a rock when Joe Williams walked past to flush. The trainer fired his pistol in the air and turned.

"Jack's bird."

The dogs were gone again, so fast that the men had to run in order to keep them in sight. The En-

glish setter found another partridge, and Mike stead-
fastly honored his point. A surprised look crept into
the trainer's face. He had expected a rough, wild
puppy, and had found a trained hunter.

Danny glanced sideways at Ross, wonder in his
eyes. The wild, unruly Mike was no more; their
rough diamond had become a sparkling, polished
jewel. True, the young English setter was two birds
up, but not by much. Had Mike been only a few feet
ahead, he would have been credited with both finds.

Then Mike gave a sudden burst of speed that
carried him toward a patch of wintergreen berries.
The red puppy was exercising his self-taught knowledge of birds, all the facts he had learned by painful
trial and error. He thought there would be game in
the wintergreen patch, and there was. The English
setter honored his point. Two minutes later Mike
found and pointed again. The red puppy had come
into his own.

Danny sighed his relief. An hour had gone past
and the score was even. Mike was holding the
champion. He glanced over at John Price, and
grinned at the anxiety on his face.

Then, for almost half an hour, there were no birds.
Racing full speed, taking turns in the lead, Mike
and the English setter investigated every likely
looking place. The English setter was the first to
strike game.

Danny's heart sank. This would make it three to
two, time was nearly up, and birds were hard to find.
The trainer went into flush.

Just then a hawk pursued his winding way through the beeches and flew directly over the birds. Four grouse burst up one by one, each announcing its rise with the thunder of its wings. They flitted among the trees like four dodging forest sprites, and at scattered points came to rest in a huckleberry bog. Danny looked questioningly at Ross, who shook his head. Undoubtedly the point belonged to the young black and white setter. It was no fault of his because the birds had flushed at the sight of the hawk.

Danny glanced at Mike. Running side by side with his wonderful rival, he headed into the huckleberry brush. The men came to the edge of the bog and peered into it.

Backed by the young English setter, Mike was on a steady point. Joe Williams flushed, and Danny saw the bird rise to wing strongly into the woods. Three to three! Never faltering, Mike started quartering at an angle.

Danny swallowed hard. He had read somewhere that Irish setters had been originally bred to hunt the Irish bogs, and Mike was certainly in his element here. More than that, he was putting to use all the experience which he had acquired running free in the woods. The young English setter hesitated, then fell back. He wanted to cast and hunt.

But Mike knew exactly where to go. He found and held another of the scattered covey, then a third, and at the far end of the bog he pointed the fourth. It was beautifully precise work, and the

English setter, by now, appreciated fully the prowess of his companion. Instead of hunting for himself, he followed Mike.

The trainer flushed the last bird, and Mr. Haggin said, "Time's up."

When the trainer whistled, the young English setter turned at once and came in. Mike looked questioningly around when Ross summoned him. Then, reluctantly, he too came in.

Danny felt Red's breath hot on the back of his hand, and turned to follow the rest as they started toward the big house. Mr. Haggin dropped back to walk beside Danny and Ross.

"You win," he said with a chuckle. "Do you want to take your Irishmen right up to the lodge? You'll find everything you need there except food. Draw on us for that, and move down from Budgegummon at your convenience." He cleared his throat. "I'd like to have you get Sean and Eileen ready for the summer shows."

Still in a happy daze, Danny heard his father's voice, as though from a great distance.

"I reckon we can," Ross said.

## ABOUT THE AUTHOR

JIM KJELGAARD spent his boyhood in country much like that described in this book. "Those mountain farms," he remembered, "produced more rocks to the acre than anything else. But they provided my brothers and me with plenty of ammunition for fighting the neighboring boys across the creek. One of our jobs was to shoo the cows out of the corn patch, which was more exciting than it sounds. There were always two or three yearling bulls in the dairy herd, and when we wanted to get home quickly, we'd each grab one by the tail. The bulls would light out for the barn, their feet hitting the ground about every two yards, and ours in proportion. But the really entrancing thing was the forest that surrounded us: mountains filled with game, and trout streams loaded with fish." Jim's first book was *Forest Patrol*, based on the wilderness experiences of himself and his brother, a forest ranger. *Big Red, Irish Red* and *Outlaw Red* are dog stories about Irish setters. His other books about dogs are *Stormy, Lion Hound, Desert Dog* and *Snow Dog*.

# Shop at home
# for quality childrens books
# *and save money, too.*

Now you can order books for the whole family from Bantam's latest listing of hundreds of titles including many fine children's books. *And* this special offer gives you an opportunity to purchase a Bantam book for only 50¢. Here's how:

By ordering any five books at the regular price per order, you can also choose any other single book listed (up to $4.95 value) for just 50¢. Some restrictions do apply, so for further details send for Bantam's listing of titles today.

---

**BANTAM BOOKS, INC.**
**P.O. Box 1006, South Holland, ILL. 60473**

Mr./Mrs./Miss/Ms. _____
(please print)

Address _____

City_____ State _____ Zip _____

FC(C)—11/85

Printed in the U.S.A.